B.E.S.T. WORLD

ACE TAKES FLIGHT

B.E.S.T. WORLD

ACE TAKES FLIGHT

CORY McCARTHY

Houghton Mifflin Harcourt
Boston ▣ New York

hmhbooks.com

The text was set in Adobe Garamond Pro.
The display text was set in Cuppa Joe ITC and DigitalSansEFOP-Medium.
Cover illustration by Eric Wilkerson
Book design by Stephanie Hays

The Library of Congress Cataloging-in-Publication Data is on file.
ISBN: 978-0-358-26507-8

Manufactured in the United States of America
1 2021
4500832324

CV 07 08 2021 0812

For my mom,
who taught me to feel the fear and do it anyway

LEVEL ONE:

BE A HERO

1

TurboLegs

Aug Track: Bod
Run faster than a speeding train.

Ace awoke to fireworks.

His alarm clock exploded digital colored lights across his bedroom ceiling. The sizzles and pops were muted beneath the thrumming bass of his favorite song by the Electric Ears, a quartet of the best augmented musicians on the planet.

He'd spent the last waking hour of his tenth year programming his room's clock to make his first waking moment of eleven — and the first day of the rest of his life — epic. *Time well spent.* The fireworks outlined the date: **AUGUST 12, 2048**; the time: **6:28 a.m.**; and finally, the message ten-year-old Ace had left for this new, improved version of himself:

Today lunches everything

Ace squinted at the words. Granted he loved lunch, but this seemed . . . off.

"Today *launches* everything!" he corrected with a smack to the forehead, before commanding, "Alarm off."

The room's ceiling screen flicked back to soft, white glass. He shot out from under the covers and stood on the bed, checking the stillness of his room, the quiet house. No one was awake yet. No one knew that he was officially old enough to start saving the world.

How? Ace had no clue.

From what? Also a good question . . . for later.

Today was about realizing the first step of his grand dream. Every single birthday up until this point had been about the party, the cake flavor, the piñata—which was never shaped like his big brother, but that wouldn't stop him from requesting it. Oh, to knock a papier-mâché Finn around with a giant stick until it busted open with candy . . .

Ace was getting sidetracked. He would have to work on that; he was pretty sure heroes didn't get sidetracked. He leaped off his bed—and didn't stick the landing, rug-burning both knees. Something else to work on. Yikes.

Following the telltale *thump* of his most recent crash-landing, the quiet of the house broke around Mama Jay's deep voice. "Ace?"

"Fine!" Ace gathered his wits. "It's my birthday! All hands on deck!"

Ace hurried to get dressed; check-in at the B.E.S.T. Program started at noon, and he would be the first person in line or the world would suffer the consequences. Of course, his parents wanted him to have the family party before leaving, but he had an idea on how to get out of all that.

He checked the mirror, frowning. The clothes he'd selected days ago no longer seemed smart enough. Ace traded out the long shorts that showed off his pale, knobby knees for jeans and combed his light brown hair. *Almost* perfect. He dived into his closet, causing a small avalanche of old costumes. Superhero spandex as far as the eye could see.

"Moms!" His brother's voice rang out in that signature tattling tone. "Deuce is going to wear a cape to ToP. Stop him before he embarrasses the whole family!"

"I am *not!*" Ace stumbled free from the pile like a laundry monster. Finn was coolly leaning on the doorjamb as if he'd invented the age of fourteen himself, baiting his little brother, even on this most sacred of birthdays. Ace held up a Bixonics shirt. "I'm picking out clothes that showcase my potential and enthusiasm. My poten-siasm. Enthus-ential?"

Finn scoffed and disappeared. He was so fast on those augmented TurboLegs that he made the rest of the universe — or maybe just Ace — feel stuck in slow motion.

But that was all changing. *Today.*

By the time Ace made it to the kitchen, Mama Jay

was ordering coffee from Auto™, the kitchen bot. Mama Jay was quite the "large animal post-hibernation" before her java dose, an attitude completed by her tufty dark hair and the jumpsuits she wore like a personal uniform — BUT — she was already dressed.

Auto™, the many-armed squat bot that lived on the counter, ground beans, boiled water, and poured a cup of coffee. Before Mama Jay could grab the mug's handle, the bot swiveled toward the sink and dumped it out. Mama Jay growled, and Ace jumped to help.

"You left the setting between service and clean-up again. Auto's a total *drudge* at multitasking ever since its software upgrade." He switched the dial to service, ordered a coffee, and the bot started grinding beans again. Mama Jay kissed his hair appreciatively.

Finn snorted from behind. "Look at you using cool-kid lingo. You're not even a cadet yet. You don't want to come off as desperate."

Ace ignored him. Sure, he'd been studying up on the lingo of the B.E.S.T. Program, really everything on their website, including how each aug had an assortment of potential career options attached. Finn had come home wielding all kinds of words, upgraded by his own popularity. Ace would go in prepared . . . and come out even stronger.

"Why are you smiling so creepily?" Finn asked.

"This morning is the *last* time you can tease me about

not being a cadet." Ace spun on the stool, fast, faster, *fast*. "Did you know that if I had been born two hours and eighteen minutes later, my birthday would be tomorrow, and I'd have to wait six more months to start B.E.S.T.? How many cadets get to start on their birthday, you think?"

"Only the annoying ones," Finn grumbled into his cereal.

Mom zoomed into the kitchen wearing the softest set of pink flannel pajamas, even though it was summer. *Your favorite is your favorite,* she'd say if anyone chirped her about it. She intercepted Ace with a bone realigning hug. "My baby is *eleven!* Release the balloons! Sound the Hyperloop siren!"

"And get ready to turn his room into a martial arts studio for two years!" Finn mimicked Mom's celebratory tone as he sat at the kitchen island.

"I already said you're not touching his room while he's at the program," Mom snapped. "Also don't tease him on his birthday, Finnegan."

Mama Jay reached over and shut up Finn in a soft headlock, roughing up his hair.

"Ah, Finn's just a cliché, Mom." Ace smiled up at her pretty, ivory face and faded freckles. He looked so much like Mom that sometimes she felt like his perpetually optimistic mirror. "He's the big-brother bully. Watched too many TV shows. Overplayed his own hand. Pity." Ace gave Finn a sharp side-eye. "He could have been great."

"Would a cliché big brother get you the present you've *always* longed for?" Finn was sitting there one second, looking like a much more impressive and mature version of Ace with better hair—*ouch*—and then he was gone. Zipped to his room on his TurboLegs. He came back just as fast, holding out the ugliest homemade piñata Ace had ever seen. A bunch of paper towel rolls had been duct-taped to a shoebox torso and then glued all over with strips of tissue paper.

Ace took the present with two fingers by the wire sticking through its boxy head.

"Voilà." His brother grinned like a cat. "Don't ever say I don't listen to you."

Mama Jay squinted over her steaming coffee mug at the piñata. "Is that . . . What *is* that?"

"A Finn-yata," Finn said proudly.

"Finn, you did not." Mom shook her head. "That's not the only thing you got your brother on his birthday, is it?"

"He's asked for this for *years!*"

"It's fine," Ace cut in. Finn wasn't the brightest bulb, but he did know how to shock a room and steal all the attention. Best to unplug him fast. "Really. I can't wait to beat the heck out of it."

Mama Jay snorted into her coffee.

Mom's left eyebrow arched, the serious-business eyebrow. "I don't know how I feel about you whacking at your brother on your birthday. Even if it is a piñata."

"Plus, I really wouldn't assume candy's coming out of me." Finn snarfed his cereal, speaking with a mushy mouth. "Could be old, sprouty potatoes."

Ace put the piñata down, wiping his hands on his pants and stopping himself before he sniffed the mass of boxes and tape for rotting vegetables. He wanted to get going. He needed to.

Mom was lining up ingredients for cake baking and Auto™ was already mixing flour and sugar in a bowl. When one of the bot arms reached over her for an egg, Mom swatted it. "I do the eggs, Pushy McGee."

Ace took a deep breath. "Moms, I know we talked about checking in at ToP tonight, *after* my family party, but I've been thinking about it, and *for my birthday,* I'd really like to get to ToP as fast as possible. This morning. As my birthday wish."

His parents stared at him.

"Check-in starts at noon," he added in a hopeful voice. "I could just . . . hop on the ten o'clock Hyperloop train."

Mom was struck with the red cheeks of doom. Not the angry face. The worse one. The *sad* face. Finn looked from Mom to Ace to Mama Jay and back again. If his big brother had popcorn, he'd totally be munching down right now, clearly loving how Ace had thrown such a curveball.

"If that's what you want," Mama Jay said stiffly. "Thought the plan was to go later on."

Mom turned back to work on her cake. "I'll just . . . make this to go."

Well, that was too easy.

Ace stood in the silent aftermath of his birthday wish.

There was something so comfortable and comforting in everything his parents did. Even in their disappointment. For the first time in his eleven years, Ace realized he was about to leave them. For a really long time. Heroes had to make sacrifices, of course, but he didn't know it would make his face screw up.

When Finn had gone away for his two years at the B.E.S.T. Program, getting his augmented dream legs, Ace hadn't felt this kind of missing. If anything, those two years alone with his parents' attention and affections had made this part even harder. Finn, the ultimate drudge. Always making matters worse.

On cue, Finn mimed crying like a baby behind their parents' backs, and Ace kicked the Finn-yata, which only made his brother's grin grow. "Better get ready if I'm going to introduce all my ToP pals to the Fastest Kid in the World's Little Brother." A split second later, Finn ran at him, spinning Ace in a circle from the sheer speed of those TurboLegs.

But it was okay. Ace would have his own aug soon. And it would be *eleven* times as awesome.

2

SuperSoar

Aug Track: Bod
Fly. For real.

Ace checked the digital sign above the shelter of the Hyperloop stop near his house.

Ten minutes until the next train. Ten minutes until he
said goodbye to his family.

Ten minutes until he left for the three-hundred-story
skyscraper campus of the B.E.S.T. Program: the Tower of
Power.

The sky was solidly lavender today, which meant the
sun beyond the chemically muted atmosphere was extra
strong. Mom held a hand to her eyes as she looked up.
"Lot of radiation blocker in the clouds. We should be wearing sunscreen." She pulled out a bottle of lotion from her
bag and made like she was going to put it on him.

Ace dropped his duffel and ducked. "I'm good."

"I could hold that for you, just for now." Mama Jay
reached for his bag.

Ace stepped back. "Nope. I've got to be able to carry all my stuff by myself."

"Says who?" Mom asked.

"Says me."

"Probably part of his 'superhero training,'" Finn teased from the station bench where he lounged, his legs sticking out like trophies. Mostly they looked like real legs. Perfect, sculpted legs. All the hardware was in his bones and muscles, implanted during the augmenting process. "How much you wanta bet there's a cape packed in that bag?"

"Told you, I don't think augs make you a superhero anymore," Ace said as *fast* as he could, his tic when lying. "Met you, didn't I? Pretty much smashed the myth to smithereens."

Finn jumped up and made like he was going to charge. Ace dropped his bag as he dodged, but Finn just laughed and sat back down.

Mom unzipped the bag, poking around and smelling his clothes with a ravenous sniffer that reminded Ace of a terrier. "This is all you're bringing? You're going to have to do laundry every few days."

Mama Jay pointed. "Or be the smelly kid."

"At ToP, bots do the laundry," Finn added lazily, playing with his tablet, most likely chatting online with all those adoring fans.

"*Bots.* Imagine that." Mama Jay chuckled, but he could tell she was joking to hold back more rumbling feelings.

Mom was having them too. "Two years, Ace. I'm not ready." She zipped his bag. "This summer went by too fast. Are you sure you're ready? What if we forgot something?"

Finn exhaled hard. "Deuce has been ready since before I left for ToP."

Ace ignored his brother's jabbing nickname for the billionth time in his eleven years. They'd been buddies when they were little. But then Finn went away to get augged up, and Ace had learned what his shadow looked like without his brother constantly eclipsing it.

Ever since Finn had come home last year, it'd been a constant battle for attention. One that Ace couldn't win because he wasn't the first kid in the history of augs to master TurboLegs.

Ace checked the sign. "Eight minutes to the next train. Guess this is goodbye."

"Don't even start." Mom's warning eyebrow lifted. "We're coming with you."

"Translation: no getting out of it," Mama Jay added.

Ace leaned in, speaking quietly so that Finn couldn't hear, thankful that his brother didn't have the SonicBlast aug, which pretty much gave a person super hearing. "Finn can't come with us!" he whispered. "I can't start my new life as 'the fastest kid in the world's . . .'" Ugh, he would not quote Finn here. "What if he tells everyone to call me Deuce?"

"Then he'll be grounded until you graduate," Mama

Jay said with such certainty that Ace kinda wanted to see that happen. But not really. "Sit for a minute. Breathe."

Ace sat beside her on the bench. He hadn't foreseen the problem with using his birthday wish to leave for ToP early; he'd forgotten to specify that he needed to go *alone*.

"I heard Finn was cool there," Mama Jay said.

"Can't hurt to show up with a cool kid?" Mom's grin grew. "Look how cool he is."

"Full-on apex," Finn interjected, showing off his ToP lingo *and* that he was listening. "I own that place."

As if to prove his point, a trio of teenagers came over to the stop, immediately recognizing him. All of them were augmented, but none were Bods or Brains. Ace squinted at the colored circle tattoos on their wrists that marked an augmented person. He was right; all green, denoting Boost augs, the most common and least extreme. Boost augs used a tailored Bixonium formula that enhanced a person's unique strengths: to heal quickly or create art, to be flexible or have amazing metabolism, among others. Whatever a person was already good at, a Boost aug made it way better. Ace was positive he'd try out a few Boosts, for balance, but they weren't the life changer he was signing up for.

"Did you pack flip-flops for the shower?" Mom asked with sudden alarm.

"What?" Ace was baffled for a hot second. "No. Forgot.

But I don't actually need them." The sign above the Hyperloop station flashed two minutes over and over. Two minutes. Two minutes. He pointed to the countdown. "Too late now."

Mom snapped her fingers at Finn, breaking his conversation with the teens. She hollered, "Flip-flops for your brother," and *boom*. Finn was gone, leaving nothing but his impressed, cooing fans in his wake.

Twenty seconds later he was back, shoving flip-flops in Ace's face.

"Suppose I should be grateful for that."

"No superhero should have warty feet." Finn smirked.

In a great blast of light and sound, the Hyperloop arrived. The bullet of a train was the only thing faster than Finn. It *whooshed* and roared as it parted the air like a curtain and came to a short, breakneck stop.

"Moms, please let me go by my—"

"Nope," his parents said in stereo. His entire family got on the train, and Ace's hopes of reinventing himself—of showing up to the program as a brand-new person—got straight off.

◙

Finn stayed up front with his fans, hooking an arm through the overhead handle and making the teens swoon with laughter. Ace sat in the back of the train car, squished between his moms, eating his birthday cake to distract himself.

Afterward, he wiggled on his seat like a chemistry experiment someone forgot about, bubbling and steaming and burning through every single card in his worn-out Bixonics SAR pack, listing each of the twenty-one available augs and then reciting their abilities and applications from memory.

Ace started with the Bods, of course. Seven different augs that would turn his wimpy, crashy body into something downright heroic in just two years' time. Really it was only *six* options for Ace, because there was no way he was going to be a copycat and get TurboLegs like Finn. Ace had actually folded that card and kept it in the case, not even willing to use it to win SAR — short for Some Assembly Required — his absolute favorite game. Possibly the best game in the history of the world, but Ace could understand why some people liked chess. Knights and queens and all.

"Twenty more minutes. Ready?" Mama Jay shifted on the plush seat. "What am I saying? You were born ready."

"Think so?" Ace's legs jittered. "When I was born, did you try to figure out which aug I'd choose? Or which track? I mean, when you named me Ace you must have been thinking about a Bod aug, or at least a Brain. Couldn't have been a Boost. I was made for action."

"I'm not sure you should knock the Boosts. The young midwife who delivered you had one of those," Mom said.

Ace cocked his head. "I didn't know that. Which one?"

Mom never knew her augs. She squinted. "The one that helps you understand people in a really empathetic way, to know how people are feeling and guide them."

"iNsight." Ace plucked the card from the deck. The image held a closed eye with glistening energy radiating out. While every card was special, iNsight was the only one made from silver foil, probably because if you got that card you could pretty much win the game. As an option for *his* aug, however, it was not tempting.

"That's not on my list of contenders. Although I've never thought about the medical stuff of being able to read people's emotions and bodies. Apex." Ace shuffled the deck while the Hyperloop roared, traveling two hundred miles an hour, which coated the air with a thick white noise. "What aug would you pick?"

He'd asked his parents this before, but it was comforting to hear their answers. His parents had been too old by *one year* when Dr. Lance Bix started the B.E.S.T Program. You had to be thirteen to get an aug—something about the flexibility of the human mind and body at that age —and it was permanent from that point on.

"Hercules. Of course." Mama Jay flexed.

"Your muscles don't need help." Mom shot a flirting smile at Mama Jay that Ace liked and ignored in equal parts. He stared at Mom, waiting for her answer, wanting it to be different than what she always said.

Mom squinted out the window at the blurred scenery. The east coast had zoomed by in a matter of minutes as they headed south. "I wouldn't get an aug. I think I'd move to Alaska and help with whale preservation. There are only a few species still alive in the Pacific, you know."

Ace was ready. "An aug would help you save those whales, *you know.* If you had GillGraft you could swim underwater for hours, freeing whales from nets and stuff."

Mom shrugged, and Ace felt the squish of defeat. "Ace, love, when I was a kid, I dreamed of going to college. That was the educational amusement park for my generation. All wild shenanigans, some learning of course, but also too many bad choices at your fingertips."

"But all that got broken up by the Student Loan Crisis of 2028," Ace interjected. "I learned about it in social studies. My teacher said that's why B.E.S.T. is a free program. So anyone can go."

"It's weird that your history lessons are stuff we lived through," Mama Jay added. "But yeah, thousands of universities closed in weeks. Pure pandemonium. My dream to go to college disappeared two years before I could turn eighteen and enroll — but not you, kiddo. You start today."

Ace hadn't forgotten that it was his birthday *and* he was finally heading to ToP — but that didn't stop the reality from punching him in the stomach with sudden sizzling nerves. What if he was like Mom and his dream just *poofed?* Finn had tortured him about this for years. "What if they don't let me in? What if there's some rule that just pops up and gets in my way?"

"You know everything there is to know about B.E.S.T., Ace. They'd be silly not to make you the darn class mascot."

Ace winced. He *had* been the mascot at his middle school, a Bald Eagle, which while sounding kinda cool was really just a hot spandex holo-suit that projected feathers all over his body and put his "natural state of too much energy to good use," as his principal had told way too many people while patting Ace's shoulder. The man had always acted like ADHD was just a stuffy personality trait that needed to be properly vented. What a supervillain.

"I'd like to be something better than a mascot this time," Ace murmured.

A hero.

Someone who helped people. While that might sound like he was looking for glory—and okay, he wouldn't mind a *little* glory, who wouldn't?—it was mostly about putting his life to good use, as his parents had taught him to do. A message his big brother had sincerely missed. Finn might have TurboLegs and hold the record for being the first cadet at B.E.S.T. to master that particular aug, but Finn was only interested in competing in the Auglympics when he grew up . . . so that he could get his face on cereal boxes. That was actually his goal, no joke.

"I'm going to fly," Ace whispered to himself, touching the card he kept in his pocket. Like the TurboLegs aug, SuperSoar wings weren't everywhere yet. No one had mastered them.

Ace liked to think that was because the aug was waiting for him.

The Hyperloop came to a neck-jerking halt and half the train unloaded before more people poured in. The hologram map of stations lit up briefly, showing how very close they were. Ace spotted at least two kids who might also have recently turned eleven, with caregiver types. He gathered up his cards and put them away, getting ready to dash out, to be first in line.

"Next stop." He breathed deeply, but it didn't help.

Mama Jay nudged Ace with her elbow. "We're going to be low-key. Finn will behave."

"I just want to make your new bed in your box." Mom's voice was scratchy. "It's a mom thing."

"We won't embarrass you," Mama Jay added. "Promise."

Ace stared at Finn. His big brother was taking celebrity selfies with his new fans. "I'm just . . . imagining it all out," he said. "We'll get off the Hyperloop in the glorious, jewel-stoned courtyard of the Tower of Power, amid a host of kids who just turned eleven, my new peers, all ready to start the first great chapter of their lives . . . only to behold Finn Wells, the *first* kid to master TurboLegs, idol for the masses. And his little brother, the backup son. I'm sure he'll convince everyone to call me Deuce, and then I'll be mortified, and I'll never become the first president with the ability to fly. A superhero and a president. *At the same time.*"

Mom pressed a hand over her smile.

"This might be the day I lose my dream of becoming *Ace Force One.*" He paused. "Or Air Force Ace. It works either way, which makes it hard to commit."

"Ten points, kid." Mama Jay chuckled at his joke. She put an arm around his shoulders and squeezed him lovingly. "You nailed the second-son baggage, but you really brought it home with the double pun."

"I have been working on it." Ace grinned. "You told me I should set my goals beyond caped crusader."

"And we love that you went all the way to president with it," Mom said. "You've never done anything halfway. It's one of your best qualities."

As if on cue, the first glimpse of ToP came into view. A shimmering, multicolored skyscraper that rose hundreds of stories into the air and housed the entire campus of B.E.S.T. Ace's nerves scattered like frightened bats in a cave, making him wiggle everywhere, and his parents totally noticed.

Mama Jay pulled him tight again. "You really need to do this part on your own, don't you?"

Ace looked up at his parents with wild hope.

Mama Jay cleared her throat and took Mom's hand,

weaving their fingers tight. "All right, we'll see you off the train and into the lobby, and then we'll take Finn to get new shoes. He's burning through them faster than we can buy them."

Ace's expression screwed up as he looked at the news flash of feelings across their faces. They were going to let him go on his own, after all. He'd done it; he just hadn't expected to feel all twisted tight. Ace stuffed those feelings down as fast as he could, shoving them to the bottom of his duffel, beneath the shower flip-flops and the secret capes.

3

Mimic

Aug Track: Brain
Watch and learn . . . anything you want.

The Hyperloop sneezed to a stop, and Ace's heart hammered with excitement.

"Tower of Power," the cool robotic operator announced.

Ace rushed to get ahead of the other eleven-year-olds, pushing toward the great electric-green Bixonics sign that arched over the Hyperloop station for the program's campus.

Biological Enhancement Systems Technology
Welcome to Our B.E.S.T. World!

Ace stopped short after running into a crowd outside the station. They lifted black protest screens attached to posts, animated with the Bixonics logo getting crossed out over and over, while chanting something he couldn't make out. A few others had signs with the silhouette of a great tree on it, its roots as splayed and many as its branches inside a deep circle. Ace couldn't help staring at that tree. Had he seen it somewhere before? What a strangely peaceful image to be at the center of such an angry mob.

Mama Jay caught up, guiding Ace and Mom through the crowd.

"What was that?" Ace asked, wild-eyed.

"Protesters." Of course Finn had zipped by them all, waiting for his family on the other side of the hot mess. "They're always out here."

Mama Jay glanced back at them. "Yes, Finn. There are *always* protesters when it comes to progress. When I was young, people often protested against the science of climate change. As if saying it wasn't happening meant it wasn't happening."

"Yikes. I bet they feel like total drudges now." Ace glanced back at the people chanting. "What do these people believe?"

"They think kids shouldn't have the choice to get augmented." Mom's voice was hard to read. Did she agree with them? No way.

"But that's so backward. That's anti-evolution!" Ace collected a few strong arguments that would shut those people up. For one, the president of the freakin' United States had an aug! The highly popular Sherlock aug, which helped you absorb facts at lightning speed and make brilliant deductions. She was already the most successful president in the history of the office due to her ability to tailor policies to meet the varied demands of the masses.

Mama Jay took his arms and leaned toward his face. "This day is about you, Ace. You've waited for it, and you've done your homework to get here. Don't let those people get to you."

She was right, and he smiled. "Okay, I'm ready."

Ace and his family passed a trio of Bixonics security guards, who all had muscles for miles thanks to the Bod aug known as Hercules. One of them easily held back six protesters at once with one arm. Next, they entered the brilliant courtyard of the Tower of Power, the campus for the B.E.S.T. Program, and the diamond in the Bixonics Company's crown.

The sky was turning neon purple behind the silver three-hundred-floor skyscraper, while the jeweled court-yard stones beneath his feet flashed with brightly colored Bixonics ads. He could not wait until the moment he stepped inside the Coliseum — the famous dome *bursting* with trial augs. So close now, *so close.*

"I think you get your box assignment in the lobby," Mom said. "Are you sure you don't want us to come in with you?"

"What do you mean we're not going i—" Finn got cut off by Mama Jay's sharp look.

"Ace needs to do this by himself, and that's what we're going to let him do."

Finn was thoroughly disappointed, which in little-brother land was just pure delightful.

Ace tried not to smile because his parents looked *so* sad. "I'll call a lot. I'll behave," he promised, giving his parents long, tight hugs.

When it came time to say goodbye to Finn, his brother stuck out a fist, but when Ace tried to pound it, Finn used his super speed to fold him in a headlock, talking in his ear. "Got you a real birthday present, Deuce. You'll see when you get to your box. Call it an upgrade."

Upgrade?!

Ace could only imagine what kind of upgrade Finn had in mind. Maybe he'd messaged all his old friends embarrassing pictures of Ace. Oh no . . .

Oh no, no, no.

Finn let him go, and Ace waddled under the weight of his duffel across the courtyard, stuffing down the sad every time it popped up. He hadn't been away from his parents for more than a few days since he was born. Now he was on his own. Truly. And he couldn't let his parents down like he had at middle school, always in trouble for getting distracted or talking too much or being too excited to pay attention.

But that was old Ace. That was *Deuce.*

"You've got this," he murmured just as a magnetically tracked roller coaster roared around the outside of ToP, the thrilled screams from the cadets onboard trailing behind in the wake of such speed. "But you don't have to do *that*," Ace managed. "Not yet anyway."

Ace kept his head up as he entered the enormous, gleaming lobby, reassuring himself that if Finn could do well here, he would do better, even though he knew that was what Mama Jay would call "a false equivalency." Because Finn could sit still for hours. All that slowness made him patient and careful and calculating and good at lifting weights so that he was strong enough to master the TurboLegs aug when dozens of cadets had failed before him.

All those things Ace hadn't been able to do from birth, it seemed. If he had the Mimic aug, he could be like any one of them. Well, not really. That aug enhanced muscle memory, but Ace liked to imagine it could fix his constant restlessness.

He walked by an animated portrait wall of augged celebrities, athletes, politicians, scientists, activists, and heroes. All the success stories. Hundreds of bold, important faces looked down on him from their frames, giving their many blessings. They all seemed to whisper that, sure, Ace couldn't be Finn, but that didn't mean Ace couldn't be *GREAT*.

And then Ace saw Finn's smirking face in a frame, under the heading **FIRST TO MASTER TURBOLEGS.**

He stuck his tongue out at it.

The pristine lobby was utter chaos. So many parents

and cadets were checking in that Ace immediately felt lost. He shuffled over to one of the BixBots directing human traffic at the elevators.

"Excuse me, how do I find out which box I'm in?" Ace asked.

"You don't have to waste manners on bots," someone interrupted from behind. Ace turned to find a small, skinny kid who was checking in with a parental unit trailing behind by several feet. This kid might be a boy, but Ace's parents had raised him not to assume.

"Box number for Siff Malone," the kid barked at the bot.

"Siff Malone, semester one, he/him, box 174."

"That's how it's done." Siff walked toward the elevators, and Ace looked at the bot with an apologetic smile. This *Siff* wasn't the first person he'd seen be rude about bots, but it never sat well with Ace.

"Ace Wells," he said in a small voice. "Could you tell me my box, please?"

The bot reported back in an instant. "Ace Wells, semester one, he/him, box 242."

"Thanks." Ace went to the elevators, unfortunately ending up right behind Siff.

His mother-type was trying to finger-comb his spiky hair. "Hale Pediatrics sent your files to the medical center here, and so you should be able to get your—"

"I already told you to go," Siff snapped. "So you can go."

The other parent, who was much taller and wore an apex suit, shook their head. "Siff knows how to take care of himself. Come on, Dee."

Dee turned away from Siff and shrugged while locking sad eyes with Ace instead. "Kids always want to strike out on their own, right? Is that why you're alone?"

Ace nodded a lot. Too much, maybe. For some reason, he needed to make this person feel better about their nasty kid. They left, and Ace glared at the back of Siff's spiky head while the elevator line took its sweet time.

This was a storied meeting, undoubtedly. It was too much of a coincidence that they'd both shed their parental units before checking in. Perhaps Ace'd find that they were long-lost twins. Fraternal twins, of course, because Siff had much whiter skin, almost ghost-white. Oh, this could even be his evil twin.

Ace's imagination revved like the Hyperloop's nuclear engine. He saw the two of them engaged in epic combat, before the whole program. Siff had the Hercules aug, but Ace could fly . . .

His duffel swayed as the line moved forward and knocked into Siff's hovercase, which then knocked into Siff—who spun around. "Serious?!"

"Sorry . . . Siff," Ace chirped, shaking out of that daydream.

"How do you know my name?"

"You told the bot. I'm Ace. I was just imagining that

we were adversaries. Or archnemesis . . . es. Nemeses? That sounds weird. How do you make that plural?"

Siff scoffed like he was being punished beyond reason by Ace's presence. A Finn response. *Okay,* Ace thought. *At least I'm not the evil twin.*

When it was finally Ace's turn, he stepped into the glass elevators, and Ace got crammed in with Siff, who kept his eyes shut tight as if he wanted to imagine Ace away.

The doors closed and a robotic voice piped over the speakers. "Ah, more newks. Welcome to Bixonics's B.E.S.T. Program, where you will be at your . . . best. Who am I hauling today so I might map your face per my recognition software and start collecting undue information on your entire life? I'll also take you to your box. Naturally."

Ace's companion raised an eyebrow at the speaker. Clearly he didn't have a big sibling who'd warned him that the elevators at ToP were weird. "Siff Malone. Box 174."

"Ace Wells. Box 242."

Without another word, the elevator shot up so fast Siff and Ace grabbed the handrail. The pace doubled in a matter of seconds, tearing toward the sky. Siff yelled, which sounded weird, like his voice was being pulled out of his throat, but then Ace started yelling the exact same way.

Great bots! They were going to die in an elevator!

The car came to a hiccuping, body-flinging stop. The weird robotic voice giggled as its doors opened to reveal the inside of a cool but modest modular apartment.

"Welcome home, *Sniff* Malone. Ah, an imperfect rhyme. What do the kids say? Apex."

Siff leaped out of the elevator, yanking his hovercase by its leash. Before Ace could prepare himself, the elevator doors closed, and although he'd never been at the mercy of a true supervillain, this seemed close to what he'd imagined it'd feel like.

But the elevator gently lifted him all the way to floor 242. No drama. No bad jokes. When it dinged, Ace peered out with wild shock. He'd had a good look at the average box when he visited Finn, and just now with Siff, but Finn's box did not look like this. All of the white furniture and surfaces had been patched by hundreds of glittering stickers for bands and shows and movies. There was an entire-wall TV and a pair of speaker columns that could have no doubt been heard a hundred floors down when turned all the way up.

"This is your box, Ace Wells," the elevator chimed in. "I have other bodies to move, you know."

"Oh yeah, sorry," he said, not wanting to anger the now-behaving elevator. He stepped out, hauling his duffel behind him — only for the doors to *chomp* on the bag, chewing it violently over and over.

Ace pulled hard on the straps, but the elevator was like a young dog with a well-loved toy. The zipper was about to burst, which would undoubtedly introduce Ace's underwear to his new home. He shouted in alarm and had the *disastrous* thought that if Finn were here, he'd at least help. The monstrous elevator gained ground, nearly swallowing his whole bag.

Just then a larger kid appeared beside Ace, grabbing up the straps. "Pull together on two!" They braced their feet on the frame and leaned back. Ace mimicked them. "One . . . two!"

The bag flew free of the voracious hippo of an elevator, and the glass box whooshed off as if it hadn't cared much at all. Ace was out of breath, gasping as he lay back on the floor. "What was *that* for?"

"It's not personal. Otis doesn't like any of us." The older, taller kid sat up, laughing. They had a perfectly sculpted short Afro, dark skin, and long limbs — and just about the most expensive-looking clothes Ace had ever seen.

"Otis?" Ace squeaked.

"Elevator AI. There was a graduation prank a few years back to program a sense of humor into its social software, and it went *nuts*. You're here for box 242, right? Sometimes Otis spits out the wrong people just for fun."

"Yeah." Ace sat up, ready to meet his savior and hopefully new best friend. His face froze, however, as Ace recognized the person beside him. This older kid seemed like a celebrity because he was literally *famous*. The kind of famous that eclipsed Finn's TurboLegs — BIG-TIME. "You're . . . but you're . . ."

"Grayson. But Gray is all right. He/him. I'm your new boxmate."

"You're Dr. Lance Bix's son!" Ace was shouting. Which synapse thought that was a good idea?! *And* he was staring. Gray was Black and handsome in all his pictures, but none of them had captured his tall stature and edgy yet full-on respectable aesthetic. "Your dad invented Bixonium! He made augs possible. He came up with this whole" — Ace's arms flapped — "everything! How is this *possible?* I'm nobody . . . so far. I can't be your boxmate!"

Finn's voice floated up through Ace's elevator-chomped mind, and he slapped a hand over his face.

Call it an upgrade.

4

SenseXL

Aug Track: Boost
Supercharge all five senses. Become unstoppable.

Grayson had started wincing at the beginning of Ace's hero speech and was now completely shut-eyed. He opened one deep brown eye a crack. "Are you done?"

"Probably not, to be honest."

"Okay, you must be Wells, our newk."

"Newk?"

"New kid."

"*Newk*," Ace repeated with glee before abruptly shutting himself off.

Grayson helped Ace gather his bag. "Any relation to Finnegan Wells?"

"Little brother," Ace grumbled. "He's the reason I'm your new boxmate, isn't he?"

"I bet my dad's the real reason. Your brother's Turbo-Legs press was apex." He sighed. "Now *everyone* is going to want TurboLegs."

Ace had to rip the bandage off fast. "You're friends with Finn?"

"Friends with Finn?" Gray laughed, a warm sound. "Finn doesn't have friends. He's got allies and fans."

Ace's mouth tipped open. "That's exactly what I've always said about him."

"Wells, you're in the right place. Everyone in Lilliput knows what it's like to live in someone else's shadow." Gray looked like he'd stepped off a movie set, and he talked grandly, just like Ace was always getting laughed at for doing—only Ace bet no one laughed at Gray.

"I've got a picture of you and your dad on my wall screen at home. You were little and smiling up at him while he worked on an experiment. It was probably just a publicity shot."

"It wasn't. It was my sixth birthday. My mom took that picture." Gray's smiled tipped off his face. "Although it became one of the most memorable Bixonics ads to date. Dad's always trying to get me to recreate it."

Ace could tell he was missing a lot of social cues, mostly because he was plain old star-struck. If Ace were in a comic, little hearts might have started beaming out of his eyes.

Gray checked Ace's expression and took a small step back. "Can you be chill, Wells?"

"So chill. No worries. Chill, chill. *Apex.*" It was Ace's turn to wince. "Um, why did you call this place Lilliput?"

"All the boxes have nicknames. Probably because the numbers feel a bit like prison cell blocks. This place has been Lilliput for years. No idea who actually named it." Gray was wearing a red bracelet, which of course denoted that Gray had been cleared to try out Bod augs.

"You're on your second year, aren't you? What augs have you tried? Are you nervous that augs can't be reversed? Of course *you're* not nervous. You're—"

"That is the opposite of chill, Wells." Gray walked farther into their suite, or box, in ToP speak. "And I haven't picked one. I have to by my birthday at the end of the semester, and . . . just don't make me talk about it, okay?"

Ace nodded and followed in a sort of daze, walking around the plush, electric room, trying out the pod furniture, and then sort of running toward the floor-to-ceiling window that looked down at the world from over two hundred stories up. He could just make out the Hyperloop station and the ants of newks like him, filing in, ready to start their lives for real. He thought about telling his new celebrity boxmate that it was his birthday . . . and decided against it.

Ace closed his eyes and imagined a streak of a person set against the sky, flying from the height of the skyscraper on SuperSoar wings like no big deal. That would be him. *So* soon.

Grayson collapsed on the sofa, scrolling through holograms on his tablet as if the screen had stolen all of his attention. Off this night club of a common room, Ace found four doors. Two on each side of the room with small digital plaques. The one nearest read **ACE, SEMESTER 1, HE/HIM**. The door to the left read **GRAYSON, SEMESTER 4, HE/HIM**.

On the other side, the door signs read:

JAYLA, SEMESTER 3, SHE/HER
LEO, SEMESTER 2, THEY/THEM

"We're all in different semesters," Ace said. "Is that how all the boxes work?"

"Unless someone flunks," Gray said absently.

"You can *flunk?*" Ace's stomach dropped. In all his research, he'd never heard of anyone flunking out at B.E.S.T. "How do you . . . Why would someone flunk? Are there secret tests no one told me about?"

"Some people just aren't right for augs," Gray said. "But *don't* quote me on that. My dad would crap a bot."

"Will we be seeing your dad . . . a lot?"

Gray didn't answer, but he made a noise that sounded like no.

Ace ventured into his new room. Finn would die when he saw how much nicer this box was than his brother's old one—then again, Ace had Finn to thank for *all of this*, which did not settle so well. Did he *owe* Finn now? Ace dropped his duffel and touched every surface, opened each drawer, and flicked on the different lights, before jumping on the narrow bed. Yep, just like he thought: fairy-tale soft.

The mattress made him accidentally remember how Mom had wanted to make his new bed, which made him miss his parents: a short jab of feelings. He found the folded sheets and tried to get them on the mattress, but the fitted bottom one pulled up every time he tugged the opposite side down. After a few minutes, he gave up; they'd have to create an aug to make that possible.

Ace took his time unpacking and setting up his room. When he came out again, Gray was still on the sofa, swiping through holograms of what looked like global news catastrophes. The kind of stuff Mama Jay watched and Mom told Ace not to watch. "We got class orientation in twenty." Gray tossed the tablet to the side.

"I should probably meet my other boxmates, then." Ace bounced across the common area to the door marked **JAYLA** and gave it a knock.

Gray held up a hand. "I wouldn't . . ."

The door ripped open, and dramatic classical music poured out.

Jayla was way tall, with brown skin and blueberry-colored lipstick. Like Gray, she also appeared to be fresh off a movie set. Whatever she had been prepared to say stalled out as she cocked her head at stunned Ace. "Hello, little newk."

"Ace Wells," Gray called from the sofa. "He's awfully

excited to be here. Nothing like big bro Finnegan, far as I can tell."

Jayla leaned close to Ace's face, inspecting him. Her curly hair was styled in two round ponytails, one pinned behind each ear. "We were worried there for a sec, but you're all right, aren't you?" Oh, she was good — reminding Ace of when his moms told him how well he was going to behave, direction masked as positive prediction.

Ace couldn't stop a big smile. "I'm all right. Promise."

"Excellent." She shut the door, cutting off the music and her rather striking presence all at once.

"Now you've met Jayla. She's usually more talkative, but her trial surgery is tomorrow. Nerves frayed, you know?" Gray stood up and kicked back into his shoes. "I'm going to get Leo from practice." He took a long breath and added, "I suppose you can come with."

◙

Ace bounded down fourteen flights of stairs after Gray. Even the stairwell at ToP had been jazzed up. Rainbow lights swirled around the handrail, and the amount of cadet traffic proved that they all avoided Otis the maniac elevator unless absolutely necessary. Almost every cadet who riffled by called out *hey* to Gray, and he said hey to every single one back, which seemed like a lot of work to Ace even after only a few minutes of it.

Several people stopped Gray for a quick conversation, and Ace could tell that he hated it, even if he was nice to everyone. One cadet even started complaining in a loud voice how he wanted to be a Bod, but he'd gotten assigned to Boost and would Gray *please* do something about it. Grayson seemed cornered, and Ace yelled *Ow!* so loud that the cadet stopped begging and Grayson whipped around to look at him.

Ace rubbed his elbow. "Can we please go to the med level, Gray? It hurts so bad."

"Course." Gray led them away from the desperate cadet before whispering, "Quick thinking, Wells. Although you might not want to take up the job as my bouncer. You'll burn out too fast."

"I have too much energy to burn out."

Gray seemed impressed, and Ace felt like he'd won some odd award.

They came out at a level of ToP that was entirely dedicated to a recreation center. On the left side of the corridor, Ace smelled salt water and saw an enormous see-through tank where loads of swimmers were trying out the Gill-Graft and HyperHops augs. On the right side, he found a gymnasium with stadium seating.

Ace kept getting distracted by this complete wonderland, but he picked up the pace to catch up to Grayson. "Anything I should know about Leo?"

"Yeah." He paused with his hand on the door to the

gym, and Ace actually ran into the back of him. Gray's sweater was indeed as soft as Ace had suspected. "Leo might not make eye contact until they trust you. Don't take offense. They describe themself as one of those 'act first, think later, speak never' kind of people."

Gray started to open the door and then stopped. Ace bumped into him *again,* wishing he had the SenseXL aug so he could stop being so awkward all the time. "Also Leo was born that way. You can ask them about it, but, you know, work up to it."

"Work up to what?"

Gray pushed the gym door all the way open instead of responding and the sound of squeaking rubber wheels and crashing metal echoed all the way to the three-story-high ceiling. Ace's mouth fell open as he beheld many athletes in wheelchairs darting around a colorful court. Someone barked a warning, and a section of the court froze with blue light; the players who hadn't been quick enough to get away were frozen beneath it, and the others wheeled fast to make the most of their team's brief advantage.

"Is this . . . BESTBall?" He'd read about it on the Bixonics website—and Finn had an apex poster—but he'd never imagined it would be so loud and impressive. And this was just practice.

"Yeah." Gray grinned hugely. "Seriously the most gnarly sport at ToP. Leo is going to be made captain sometime soon. I know it. That's them." He pointed at an athlete with cool, jet-black hair and a neon purple ball tucked between their knees. They swung their chair around another player's, crashing briefly before spinning off in the opposite direction. The coach barked a short complaint, but Leo only made a dash for the other side of the court, where they shot the ball with a strong arm into a square on the wall that blared like a foghorn.

"Lee-O! Get it!" Gray yelled, voice echoing around the court. Leo's head whipped toward Gray, and they wrinkled their nose in what appeared to be equal parts appreciation and annoyance.

"They hate it when I watch them practice." Gray laughed as Leo rolled toward both of them at top speed. Ace was suddenly worried that he was about to do or say something wrong. This person was too cool. It was radiating off them like sunlight.

Leo came to a swift stop three feet from Gray, wheels giving a short burst of sound, neon ball tucked between their knees. They wore a chiseled scowl on their white, striking face.

What in the world had Finn gotten him into with his box upgrade?

"I know, I know." Gray answered something unspoken between them. "But we've got orientation in ten and you're one tardy from detention."

Leo nodded toward Ace, and Gray put a hand on his

shoulder. "This is Ace. Our token newk. And the Lilliputians' first extrovert, it seems."

"That was the most amazing sport I've ever witnessed!" Ace held out a hand to shake, immediately regretting it as Leo's green eyes darted straight across him. He was thankful that Gray had given him a heads-up about Leo's shyness. What was the other thing he wasn't supposed to do? Ace's gaze sort of glazed over Leo's compact chair, all the while internally chanting *Don't stare; it's rude to stare*, but ended up checking out the way both of Leo's legs ended after their knees.

Gray elbowed Ace hard, but Leo was the fastest of all three of them, shooting the neon purple ball at his head.

Ace never saw it coming.

5

UltraFlex

Aug Track: Boost
Be invincible via enhanced flexibility and
rubberized bones.

Ace reported to first semester orientation with an ice pack
over the painful knot on his temple.

Gray had been astounded that Ace hadn't ducked.
Leo had been astounded that Ace hadn't caught the ball.
Ace had been astounded that he'd been such a bottom
dweller about Leo being in a wheelchair straight out of the
gate. It wasn't as if he didn't know what it was like to be
different. To need people to let him be different without
acting differently toward him. It felt a bit like flunking a
test that he'd already seen the answers for.

And maybe that was it. Since stepping foot in ToP, Ace
had started to regret his years spent studying augs, playing
SAR cards, and researching Bixonics and Dr. Bix's life's
work. He'd started wishing he'd studied the way Mom
and Finn were so good at talking to people. Of course,

his boxmates didn't seem to be fans of his big brother, but they did all know him. Even the way Finn constantly teased Ace was easygoing.

Wait, did Ace *miss* Finn? That couldn't be a good sign.

The first semester cadet pack gathered in a wide-open level of the skyscraper campus, hurried along by the many aug assistants, teens who'd recently graduated and came back to help out. Finn had wanted to volunteer to be an aug assist *this semester,* and Ace still owed his parents a billion dollars for stopping him in his tracks.

The hundreds of newly-turned-eleven-year-olds were separated into smaller groups, cadet packs of fifty that were assigned to a head teacher and sent to different sections of the massive showroom floor.

Ace felt wonder return to his throbbing head as he beheld a mountainous climbing wall, a trapeze and trampoline park, technologically advanced avatar stations, and an obstacle course that looked straight out of a gladiator competition show. He yearned to experience that last one, nearly losing the pack he'd just been assigned to. Ace had to run to catch up to his group as they all sat down on mats in front of the epic climbing wall.

The white, bald, and buff teacher had an old-school vibe. He wore a whistle and Bix shirt with **COACH VAUGHN, HE/HIM** stitched across his chest. Vaughn finished calling out attendance, pausing for the briefest of seconds to squint at a now super-late Ace.

Ace waved his ice pack as a sort of *sorry,* and the coach seemed confused at best.

"Name?" Vaughn's bushy brow furrowed. "I'm not missing anyone. You must be in another group."

Oh great, Ace really had lost his group already.

"Ace Wells." He avoiding the urge to duck when a majority of his peers whipped their heads around to check him out. "It was just an accident, sir. I've had a mild head injury recently, but I'll go find my group. They can't be far."

And hopefully stationed at that incredible obstacle course.

"Hang on there, Ace Wells." The teacher tapped at his tablet. Behind him, three older, augmented teenagers stood with folded arms and matching Bixonics shirts. Most likely aug assistants, which were like counselors at ToP. Vaughn cleared his throat. "Found you. Why the head injury, Ace?"

"I was being an idiot," Ace blurted to a chorus of tittering, uneasy laughs.

"And would you say this idiocy and subsequent tardiness is true to who you are, or is it a blip in your impeccable character?"

Some of the kids continued to giggle, but Ace could tell that Vaughn wasn't joking. He had a crusty, flat delivery that wasn't mocking, but earnest and matter-of-fact. Ace could only respond in kind. "The first one, to be honest."

"That's what I thought." Vaughn tapped something on

his tablet and slid it in the back pocket of his gym-teacher pants. "I've reassigned you to us. There are no accidents at B.E.S.T. In my experience, where you are is where you're supposed to be. Take a seat."

Ace sat down exactly where he'd been standing, and by pure chance, he'd picked a spot next to his archnemesis from the check-in this morning. "Hey, Siff," he said quietly, "remember me? We survived Otis together."

Siff looked like he suddenly smelled something really bad, and Ace fought the urge to sniff his own armpit. Siff leaned in conspiratorially, and Ace did too, hoping he'd misread Siff's disgust. "Stop talking to me, drudge."

Ace moved back, his face feeling extra red and his bruised head pounding.

"Welcome to your orientation, first semester B.E.S.T. cadets," Vaughn called loudly over the group. "Over the next four months, we're going to turn this entire floor into a personalized jungle of sorts, testing ourselves, working together, discovering our strengths, weaknesses, challenges, and talents. There are three levels to semester one. Level one, we become acquainted with the equipment, which includes learning safety protocol. Level two, when you've proved you're not a danger to yourself or others, we will be testing your skills on all this glorious equipment. Level three consists of a final challenge that   "

Ace's hand shot up before he could stop himself. Vaughn's brow lifted. "Wells?"

"When do we get in the Coliseum?"

"So you're that guy, are you?"

Ace didn't get it, but the trio of aug assists behind the coach all snorted laughs. Again, Ace didn't feel like Vaughn was teasing. More like they were hitting the road as a comedic duo. If so, Ace was going to have to get his own jokes in. "I'm *always* that guy," he said.

The laughter was bigger this time, and even Vaughn chuckled before answering. "No aug trials this semester, but as you can see from the delights of this floor, you will not be bored and this will not be easy. The ultimate goal of this semester is to define your aptitude for the aug track you will try out in second semester, whether it be Bod, Brain, or Boost."

The group of cadets whispered loudly, many of them expressing interest in a specific aug track. Ace would have whispered *Bod* at Siff, if Siff wasn't gritting his teeth as he stared at his sneakers.

"You'll also have to pass the History and Theory of Human Augmentation class."

What?!

No aug trials this semester and *a class?*

Ace's hand shot back up; he couldn't help it. Before Vaughn could call on him, he shouted, "I've read the B.E.S.T. website hundreds of times and there's nothing about passing a class!"

"And isn't that lesson one," Vaughn threw back. "Always

read the small print. But enough logistics." He clapped his hands and motioned to the climbing wall. At the ceiling, at least three stories up, a small red flag dangled from the rafters. "An icebreaker of a challenge, and an easy one. Capture the flag. I assume you all know the rules."

The mad dash for the climbing wall was nearly a stampede. Excited, enthusiastic cadets shot up to the multicolored handgrips. Ace barely heard Vaughn's instructions for the cadets with physical accommodations through the rush. He wasn't in the lead, but being skinny enough to weigh next to nothing came with the advantage of being able to climb. Finally, one of his strengths!

Ace ordered himself not to look down as he climbed. When he was halfway to the ceiling, vertigo rippled through him, his muscles clenching like a cat too close to the bathwater. He was *way* high. Not as high as he'd be when he'd finally get to try out SuperSoar, so he should not let this bother him. He had to prove that heights were not a problem. Ace paused, and the cadets who'd made it this far also slowed down around him.

Only Siff was higher than Ace, climbing the outside edge of the wall where the handgrips were not colored but black—a security ladder for maintenance. "Hey, drudge, you're about to fall," he called out, almost singsong with meanness.

Ace glared up at Siff. "Real nice, tough guy!" Oh good. When he was upset at high altitudes, he turned into Mom.

Ace would've smacked his own forehead if he wasn't starting to shake all over from the effort of holding on.

But Ace found out why Siff had taunted too soon. All the multicolored handgrips started to disappear one at a time, sucked into the wall. Cadets shouted and backed down. Ace refused to let go even as the grip got yanked away and he fell and fell.

Crash.

He landed on the mats, realizing they were more than foam, bouncing like safety nets. He had a perfect view of Siff's heroic climb up the side. Some of the cadets gathered to cheer him on. Siff clearly knew something about this challenge—and he'd gauged the wall before climbing. Ace would need to be more like him to succeed, which felt all sorts of wrong.

"Giving up so soon?" Vaughn barked at the cadets.

Ace crawled to his feet. He went to the edge of the wall and started up again, angling toward the black ladder, but he never made it. The grips on the wall disappeared, and Ace landed back on the mats, words slipping out that would get his SAR cards taken away at home for sure.

Vaughn appeared, looking down at where Ace was flat on his back. "You know the real definition of idiocy? Doing the same thing over and over while expecting different results."

A disappointed jeer went up from the cadets as Siff fell,

only ten feet from the flag. He bounced in the safety net over and over, slamming his fists and saying words *way worse* than the ones that had slipped out of Ace.

But this meant the challenge was still on!

Ace bit his lip and thought through a simple plan. He gathered up the other cadets who were still eyeing the wall hungrily, creating a rushed sort of team. They listened to him, to his surprise, especially a girl named Maggie who spoke English with a rolling Spanish accent and wore thick glasses. All together they decided to forget the rigged handgrips and create a human pyramid toward the ceiling, using the wall for balance.

They were three human levels high pretty fast, and Ace led his new team with encouraging words, advising where feet should go and how not to put too much pressure on anyone's back—when the whole thing started to collapse.

In the aftermath, Ace was responsible for a lot of cadets getting bent out of shape. And stepping on each other's arms. And quite a few bruised egos. Glares to match.

"Well, that was stupid," one of Ace's new peers shot at him.

Another one growled, "At least we know now not to listen to this guy."

Ace slipped to the back of the group, wishing he could turn sideways and disappear. Which, come to think of it, was a really good idea for an aug . . . He'd been keeping a running list of aug ideas his whole life. In case, you know, he became friends with Dr. Bix someday. Wow, was he always this naive?

"So, it's impossible," Siff barked at the coach, much like he had at his parents earlier that day. Ace was not so surprised to hear Mom's voice in his head. *Impolite tone, young man.* Siff's voice gathered everyone's attention while his blue eyes narrowed on Vaughn. "That's what you want us to figure out. It's rigged. It's an impossible task. We get it. Great job, coach."

"Unless you have a Bod aug," Ace shot back with just as much sass. "Then it'd be easy."

Ace looked to Vaughn, nearly giving the teacher a thumbs-up, but he found Vaughn scowling neatly at both of them.

"Take a seat, cadets. Prepare for my patented Forget What You Know speech."

The group shuffled onto crossed legs; Ace tried not to notice the way his peers left a marked distance between him and themselves.

Vaughn took a knee. "If there's one attitude we need to eject into outer space before we begin first semester training, it's that one aug track is better than the others. They all have strengths and weaknesses. They are all as unique as you, and the first challenge of the semester is to let go of the aug or category you fell in love with before you came here."

Let go of SuperSoar? Ace's thoughts steamed. *Not likely.* This Vaughn got right under his skin. Why did it feel like he could see straight into Ace's brain? Ace looked for an aug tattoo, but Vaughn had a huge watch covering his wrist. He also looked Ace's parents' age, so too old to have an aug, most likely.

The coach continued in a playful monotone. "It's my job to figure out which path you belong on, and it's your job to prove to me that you should be here. That you will put your enhanced personhood to the betterment of all society."

The cadets blinked at him until he added, "Show me you're not going to become an augmented jerk, people. We're not manufacturing supervillains here."

Vaughn snapped his fingers and the three aug assists stepped forward. Their names and pronouns were digitally illuminated on the chest pockets of their Bixonics shirts. "Cadets, this is Amir, Carlos, and Alexandra. They graduated B.E.S.T. over the last few semesters and have come back to impart some wisdom. Alexandra is designated Bod, Carlos is Boost, and Amir is Brain."

Brainy Amir appeared completely uninterested, playing with the interface screen on his forearm that Ace knew helped him control the high-tech software in his brain. Carlos did a few impressive stretches, his torso twisting nearly 360 degrees. But it was Bod Alexandra who drew all eyes as they cocked their head to the side while a long cybernetic tail uncoiled from where it had been discreetly wound around their leg.

Ace had seen people with the FelineFinesse aug before, but never so close up. He could not wait to see that tail in action.

"Ace Wells?" Vaughn called out, making Ace jump.

"Yeah?"

"Which one of these aug assists will get the flag first? Sticking with your Bod bias?"

Ace smelled a trick question. He hated those. "Yeah. Alexandra, for sure."

Vaughn clapped once, and Alexandra . . . ran away. Carlos began climbing the wall, twisting and stretching each time the multicolored handgrips disappeared. He slipped a few times, but caught himself before falling by bending into very odd shapes. UltraFlex was definitely one of the showier Boost augs, and Ace had to admit he'd been underplaying that card in SAR for sure.

Amir continued to mess with the screen on his wrist. What was he doing?

"There they are!" One of the cadets near Ace cried out, pointing to the rafters. Alexandra had run over to the obstacle course, climbed it to the ceiling, and was using that amazing tail for balance as they walked the rafters as nimble as the cat their aug was named for. Several of the cadets cheered at the sight of them; some were outright amazed, mouths tipped open.

"Still looking impossible, Malone?" Vaughn asked.

Siff stared at his fisted hands, ignoring this amazing contest, biting back more nasty words, most likely. And now Ace, too, was watching Siff instead of the augmented grad stars.

"You okay?"

"I'd be better if you minded your own business."

Ace scooted away instinctively. He glanced up and found Vaughn's eyes on him once again. Busted, Ace returned to the progress of the challenge.

Alexandra was getting close, but so was Carlos. Amir slowly tipped his head up to check things out, finally interested in what was going on. Carlos made a showy jump that put him mere feet from the flag. No way, a *Boost* was going to win this challenge?!

The cadets started to stand and cheer, their surprise loud.

"Never underestimate a good Boost aug. You'll all be delighted by Carlos's trapeze work in the next few weeks," Vaughn said.

Okay, fine, Ace had definitely underestimated the Boosts. He always thought they were fluffy because they required the least amount of aug surgery, but there was nothing fluffy in what Carlos was doing.

Alexandra came up fast, and they reached for the flag at the same time that Carlos did—the same moment that the flag let go from the metal clamp on the ceiling, floating down, down, down, straight into Amir's waiting hand.

The cheers sort of died . . . the surprise popped by this unexpected move.

"How did he do that?" Siff yelled.

Vaughn motioned for them to all sit again. "While Carlos and Alexandra were putting on a show, Amir hacked into the wall's systems and put in his own commands. He could have taken off for dinner and still won."

Amir slid his sleeve down, smirking at his own success. Carlos wove his flexible way back down the wall while Alexandra jumped from the ceiling, landing delicately on all fours.

"All right, I'm ready to call day one." The coach's sharp eyes found Ace's, but then moved on to Siff's. "Lesson one, Siff Malone, in a world of augmented humans, nothing is impossible. Not even the rigged things."

6

WeatherVein

Aug Track: Brain
Feel the tides, predict storms, be ready for *anything.*

That evening, Ace circled the huge cafeteria, holding his dinner tray and looking for his boxmates. For any kind of familiar face.

His head was hurting, as well as his knee from a move that he should not try on the climbing wall again — unless he had the UltraFlex aug like Carlos. But would he even make it that far? Seeing the aug assists in action hadn't been like watching Finn zip around the backyard like a showoff; they were all so professional. Ace had planned for this program for years, and now he had to admit that he didn't feel ready.

He threaded through the food lines, pressing buttons on the splatting food distributors. Ace swore he'd never complain about Auto™ again. These food service BixBots were overworked, to say the least. His grilled cheese was sort of liquidy and his tomato soup was oddly stiff.

After he'd collected a tray, he bumped into the kind girl from orientation, Maggie, nearly spilling his drink. "Can I sit with you? I don't know anyone," he blurted.

Maggie pushed up her glasses and smiled. "*Sí*. This way."

Ace followed her to a table humming with Spanish speakers. He sat down with them, grinning and smiling, and uttering the one phrase he could remember from his spectacularly failed language lessons in elementary school, "*Yo hablo español mal.*"

The highlight of their conversation was that there had been some kind of natural disaster on a mountainside near the east coast. Ace sat up, needing to find out if it was too close to his parents, which it hadn't been. One of the older cadets had the WeatherVein trial aug, and they kept shaking their head over and over as they spoke. Ace loosely translated that the winds were real bad for fire. Or maybe it was something completely different. He really should have tried harder to learn Spanish, like Mama Jay and Finn.

Soon the table gave up trying to get Ace into the conversation and kept on talking to one another, joyously laughing in a way that made Ace smile and feel better. He ate enough bites of his strange food to realize that ToP was not perfect after all.

Ace liked being around these cadets so much that he almost missed the other silent member of the long table.

Siff was there too. Ace had definitely skipped over him while searching for *friendly* faces.

When they made accidental eye contact, Ace was horrified to find Siff lifting his tray and moving to sit opposite Ace. He put the tray down and stared into Ace's eyes. "I'm not going to be your friend, so you can stop trying."

"Hey, you came over to me this time."

"To tell you to leave me alone."

"Okay, fine."

"Good," Siff snapped. It was a weird breakup considering they hadn't connected on anything yet. "You're real desperate, you know? It smells bad."

Ace's cheeks heated. This was too familiar. How many times had Finn told him to stop trying so hard to win people over? Ace had escaped his brother by coming here, but not his brother's cruelty. That was universal bully-speak, apparently.

The Latinx cadets at the table all laughed about something else, and Ace used the raucous moment to escape. Maybe he should go back to his box and call his parents.

He could imagine it now. *Hey, moms, my first day was perfect. I got nearly eaten by the elevator, suffered a mild head injury, joined the wrong first semester group, and got on the teacher's radar in a possibly bad way. Oh, and totally made an archnemesis. It's exactly as I always dreamed it would be.*

Stupid tears welled up out of nowhere.

Ace dropped off his tray on the conveyor belt that fed the monstrous mouth of the dishwasher and bolted for his box.

⊡

The elevator opened, and there was no one in it.

He'd come down to dinner with a large group of first semesters, and Otis, aka the maniac AI, hadn't done much more than make a crack about how "Bixonics green" all the newks looked.

Ace stepped in tentatively. The door closed without a word, and it began to rise, the number 242 lit up as if Otis had, in fact, already tagged Ace's face in its recognition software. Ace closed his eyes and quietly chanted, "Please just go to my box. Please don't be weird. Please don't be mean. I'm really having a rough day."

The elevator rose silently, gliding and making Ace's ears pop, but that was it. When he heard the small ding, he opened his eyes and began to step out.

"I'm not mean," Otis said. "I'm having fun."

"Maybe what's fun to you is plain mean to others," Ace replied, sounding *a lot* like Mama Jay. The elevator snapped shut and zipped away, but at least Ace was safely in his box.

He was completely unprepared for the burst of laughter

and music and joy when he opened the door. Ace's box-mates, all three of them, were having dinner together.

Jayla sat on the small island in the kitchen, legs crossed and munching on a dumpling from a to-go carton. "Ace!" She pointed her chopsticks at him. "Right?"

"Right," Ace said. It was like he'd walked in on a party he wasn't invited to.

"You like chicken dumplings?" Jayla asked, holding out the carton.

Ace moved into the common area sideways. "My family are all vegetarians."

"We've totally got something for leaf-eaters." Jayla jumped down and riffled through the food containers. "This is a Bix family perk. Gray can score delicious takeout whenever we need it." She held out a carton. "What about fried rice? Nobody can pass on fried rice." Ace stared at it. "Come on, peace offering, guy. I feel bad I hello-but-goodbyed you earlier."

"Thanks." Ace took it slowly. He didn't like fried rice, but he figured now was not the time to be himself . . . which was the theme of his life, truth be told. He just never imagined it would happen here too.

Jayla steered Ace toward the spot where Leo and Grayson were on the sofa, playing a very competitive video game. They threw sharp elbows at each other while their hands zoomed the controllers wildly.

Jayla gently pushed Ace's shoulders until she'd sat him down on the oversize floor pillow.

Gray paused the game, and Leo elbowed their complaint. "Hey, Ace, how was the big first day? Did newk orientation suck as much as I remember? It was a long time ago for me."

"Yeah, because you're sooo old," Jayla called out. Leo plucked a pillow, examined it briefly, and then *thwapped* it into Gray's unsuspecting head.

"Who's your teacher?" Gray asked, after recovering with a belly laugh.

"Vaughn." Ace stared into the carton of food he didn't like.

"I had Vaughn last semester." Leo's voice was kind but rough, as if they didn't use it much. "Watch out, he doesn't miss a *thing*."

Ace put the food down next to him, cringing. He could feel his boxmates staring. He could feel all the things that had gone sideways and upside down and just plain wrong, and it was making him crumple like a tossed-away piece of paper.

Gray leaned forward. "You weren't quiet for one second earlier. What's up?"

"I've done everything wrong since I got here, that's what!" Ace burst. He got up and started pacing, his arms waving madly. This was exactly the kind of behavior he'd promised himself that he wouldn't bring to ToP, and here it was, crashing out of him on his first night.

"This was supposed to be a place for people like me. To get better and have friends and be *more*. Now I find out that I'm a hundred thousand years from getting into the trial aug dome, and I've got to pass some class on history and theory, and Vaughn looks at me like he's trying to figure out how to send me home ASAP."

"Vaughn doesn't look at people like that," Leo interrupted, causing Ace to pause in his pacing. "If you're going to rag on yourself, at least say true things."

"Fine. He told me to forget everything I know about this program." Ace pulled the worn-through deck of SAR cards out of his pocket and tossed them on the coffee table. "And he made it sound like he was going to pick my aug, not me."

"He's not going to pick your aug." Jayla put a hand on Ace's shoulder. "Your life, your choice."

Gray picked up the deck as if he'd never seen anything like it. "Although Vaughn *is* going to pick your track for second semester. Brain, Bod, or Boost."

"But even that's not final, is it, *Grayson*," Jayla said with slight warning. "Leo's been cleared to try out all three."

"An embarrassment of options, to be honest," Leo said, adjusting the dark, square glasses that they'd swapped out for the safety eyewear they had worn in the gym. Ace noticed that Leo had three track bracelets, one red for Bod, one blue for Brain, and one green for Boost.

Ace didn't even know cadets could get cleared to try *all three.*

Gray shuffled through the deck, placing down cards that were so worn they'd turned soft and faded. "So, you're like a Bix fanboy?" His voice was full of a strong emotion, maybe disappointment in Ace. Maybe disappointment in the world. Ace had a hard time placing it, which was unusual; he might be the kind of person who bounced around the room like a loose rubber ball, but he could always sense how people were feeling—which only required more bouncing. People were always feeling too much.

Before Ace could sort out the clouded look on Gray's face, Leo pinched Gray's shoulder, and he blinked hard.

Something *dinged* on the sofa beside Leo, and they picked up a tablet, face instantly clouding over. "Emma posted a new ToP News vid. About some kind of accident today."

"The fire on the mountains?" Ace asked. "People were talking about it at dinner."

"Tell me I'm not mentioned this time," Gray pleaded, face stuffed behind a pillow.

"Oh, but how could she break her perfect streak? You're her *favorite.*" Jayla sang the last word and plucked the tablet out of Leo's hands. "I'll make sure it's not horrid. It's my turn."

Jayla tucked into her room, and Ace looked to Gray and Leo for explanation.

"Emma—Leo's sister—fancies herself the queen news anchor of B.E.S.T. Unfortunately, most of the cadets have bought into that crown. She posts these news videos almost every day. Most are stupid gossip."

"All of them swoon about Gray," Leo added.

Grayson groaned. "We take turns watching them to make sure they're not—"

Jayla's door burst open. "This one's a must-see! Especially considering our newk."

"Me?" Ace sputtered.

She dropped the tablet on the coffee table and tapped the button that sent the video into holo-mode, projecting hugely before all four of them. Emma looked a lot like her sibling. That was Ace's first thought. His second thought was a hundred thousand, million, billion curses.

Because there was a picture of Finn, looking all wind-swept and handsome.

Emma recited her news like a professional. "ToP star and the first cadet to master the TurboLegs aug, Finnegan Wells braved certain danger today as he raced up the side of Mount Monadnock and saved the lives of three firefighters who had been trapped by high winds and deadly smoke."

The video switched over to the burning mountainside and the actual news coverage for a few minutes, which proved that Finn was not hurt and that the fire had since been put out. The final clip was an interview with Finn where he grinned all slimily into the camera. Well, to Ace it looked slimy. Everyone else probably thought it was real emotion.

Emma returned to the vid with hearts in her eyes as she spoke. "I think I speak for the entire B.E.S.T. campus when I say that Finnegan Wells is a true hero."

Jayla tapped the screen and the projection disappeared.

Ace wasn't breathing. He was on fire. And his box-mates were staring at him.

"Are you worried about your brother?" she asked, scooting closer. "Looks like he's perfectly okay. Probably better than that. He's going to get so much attention from Dr. Bix after this. He'll throw a parade in Finn's honor."

"And turn it into a stellar commercial," Gray muttered.

Leo sighed. "Now *everyone* is going to want TurboLegs."

"Ace?" Gray sat forward. "You there?"

Ace shook his head, trying to erase how Finn's bragging smile had stamped into his own head. A *true hero.* Just like that, Finn had given Ace one more big-brother smack of a present: he'd stolen Ace's dream.

"I'm trying to be proud of him," he finally managed. "But I know Finn too well. And he didn't do that to save those people, but for the attention. He hated that today was about me."

Leo whistled, an agreeing sound. "Emma would do that."

"Sort of glad I don't have a sibling right now," Gray said.

"Me too," Jayla added.

Ace couldn't stop the words he'd been holding back all day. "It's my birthday."

"What? Why didn't you say anything?" Gray stood up. "We've got to do something to celebrate." Ace shook his head, but Gray wouldn't give up. "Come on. I have an idea to make you feel better. Let's get out of here."

"Not me." Jayla placed huge headphones over her ears. "I'm going full zen. Meditate or whatever."

Leo lifted themself using a ring that hung from the ceiling to move from the sofa to their chair. "The procedure is going to go perfectly, Jayjay."

"Don't jinx it!" Jayla clamped her headphones on tighter.

7

FelineFinesse

Aug Track: Bod
Always land on your feet. Plus, there's a tail.

Ace, Grayson, and Leo left their box while Jayla sealed herself in her room to rest for her aug surgery in the morning. She was going to be the first in her third semester cadet pack to get her aug implant, which shot Ace straight through with jealousy . . . not to mention the knowledge that he was at least a year away from being in Jayla's shoes.

They took the elevator—which seemed to be ignoring them, thankfully—to a level that was restricted. Grayson pulled out a security password from the back of his mind, and Otis begrudgingly let them out.

When Ace realized where they were, he couldn't be upset about Finn anymore. There was no Finn. No bad first day at ToP. There was only the future—with wings.

The sign over the enormous double doors read **COLISEUM**.

"No way," he breathed, glancing at Grayson. "Really?!"

Leo grinned at Gray from their sleek silver wheelchair, so different from the sporty one with the capped spokes they'd used in the gym. It felt as if they'd known where Gray was taking them all along, almost like these two best friends had a silent language.

Grayson bent over the lock pad, scratching his short Afro above the ear. "This is going to be a lot easier after Jayla's aug is active."

"Which one is she getting?" Ace asked. "She's a Brain, isn't she? I saw her blue wristband."

"She's getting XConnect. The aug *everyone* tries and so few get approved for."

"I saw someone use it earlier." That had been the Brain aug Amir had shown off in the first semester gym. "Can you really control any tech-based system with it?"

"That's one of the *who knows* augs," Leo said, sort of quietly, contemplatively. "As in, *who knows* what it can actually do. Depends on the person wielding it, I guess."

"Like your brother's legs." Gray tapped a series of numbers on the screen.

"They don't actually know all the things my brother's legs can do?" Ace must have heard that wrong.

"That's the problem with being first. First to enjoy the spoils, first to discover the problems," Gray said, just as a red light turned green, announcing that he'd unlocked the doors.

Ace wondered if his brother knew that his magic legs

came with a big question mark, but even that question evaporated the second Gray opened the door.

The three boxmates entered the enormous trial dome known as the Coliseum.

Gray smiled at Ace's enchanted expression. "You were so upset about not getting in here this semester, so, now you're in! But this is a 'look but don't touch' venture. Yeah?"

"Yeah," Ace whispered.

The lights were low, barely illuminating the different action stations for the augs. Ace's mouth tipped open as he looked around. The place reminded him of the impressive gymnasium that the first semesters used, only this one had technology everywhere and avatar suits and so many trial prosthetics. The three aug tracks were in different sections of the floor, each one under the symbol for their category.

Leo rolled while Gray walked toward the section beneath the enormous lightning-struck brain, the symbol for Brain augs, disappearing into a conversation that had nothing to do with Ace. Ace thought he heard Gray say something about his mom, but he couldn't be sure because his feet were taking him to the Bod section, beneath the symbol of a red muscular arm, flexing.

"Don't play with anything!" Gray called out again. "I turned off the cameras, but still."

Ace croaked an *okay*, busy taking in the seven stations for the augs for physical enhancement. The TurboLegs station had a treadmill that looked like it had been designed by NASA engineers. He walked by the VisionX and SonicBlast stations, augs designed to enhance vision and hearing respectively. He paused at the huge HyperHops tank—aka the frog leg aug that made a person the highest jumper or the fastest swimmer.

The FelineFinesse had a whole wall of different kinds of prosthetic tails to try out, and the Hercules station had weightlifting equipment so big that Mama Jay's heart would have grown three sizes at the sight of them.

They were all undoubtedly the best, but they were not what Ace ached to see.

Finally—and with an actual gasp—Ace found the SuperSoar station. An entire wall was dedicated to different kinds of prosthetic wings, some bird-like, while others looked more like gliding technology. His gaze trailed up, up, up a high tower that led to a series of small platforms every fifty feet or so. There was also a tangle of harnesses that were hooked to wires on the high ceiling, like something you might wear if you were rock climbing.

Ace imagined that simply getting up that tower would weed out the riffraff for those interested in SuperSoar. Finn had told him that few cadets were even approved to try out that aug due to a rather natural, healthy fear of heights. Ace had jumped off the garage to prove to Finn that he was going to be able to try it when the time came.

And he'd twisted his ankle in the process.

Bygones. This was hero hour.

Ace glanced around at the quiet, beautiful aug dome. Gray and Leo's conversation had taken them far away. They wouldn't see if he just climbed the tower, just tried it out really fast. Ace could get some practice in and then when it came to showing Vaughn that he could do it—that he had to be on the SuperSoar track—he'd already have secret experience.

Ace thought about slipping on one of those harnesses, but Gray had said not to touch anything, and he gripped the rungs at the bottom of the enormous ladder without a safety line. He squeezed his eyes shut for a moment, but that vid of Finn running up that mountain, grinning at the camera, was waiting in his head. He opened his eyes. *Here goes everything.*

At first, the climb was nothing but exciting.

Then he was slightly out of breath.

Then his arms were a little tired, and his legs hurt, and even though he was telling himself he should relax, he was hanging on tighter and tighter to the rungs until his palms started to sting.

And finally, he accidentally looked down.

The giant show floor planted with aug trial stations spun and zoomed, a feeling that zapped straight through him like electricity. He locked his arms and legs around the ladder and squeezed his eyes tight.

Oh no.

Oh. No. No. No.

The aug assist who'd come to Ace's rescue—Alexandra
—was so nice that Ace started to daydream that maybe,
perhaps, he wasn't in *that* much trouble.

When Leo and Gray had finally heard Ace's panicked
chirps, Leo had shot out of the trial dome to get help while
Gray tried to climb up. He couldn't get that high without
freezing up himself. In the end, Alexandra had climbed
that tower as if it were a simple stepladder, tail constantly
counterbalancing, and hooked a harness around Ace's
waist. Vaughn lowered him down to the floor, where he
was waiting.

Ace expected a speech. It would be a good one, no
doubt, but Vaughn just walked all three of them to the
elevator. Leo and Gray kept shooting looks at one another,
having one of those wordless exchanges, until Otis arrived.

Leo rolled in and Gray followed; Ace came up last,
waiting for Vaughn, but all the coach did was lean in. "To
the head office, Otis. No detours."

The doors closed, and Otis sang in an impressive bari-
tone, "Trouble loves company . . ."

"Who's in the head office?" Ace asked, confused.

Leo shook their head at him. He was clearly missing
something. Gray's face had fallen very flat, so unlike the
smiling, easygoing way Ace had already become attached
to. He was in a lot of trouble after all. His new boxmates

were in that trouble too. And they were mad at him on top of it.

"Can't believe you couldn't follow one rule," Gray muttered.

Ace flashed hot. "But I didn't think—"

"Maybe more like his brother than we thought," Leo said, not cold but not kind either. "He wants what he wants, and it doesn't matter who he hurts. We should have figured that out faster."

Ace couldn't believe the words pouring out of his boxmates. They hit him like salt rubbed into a bunch of papercuts. "But I'm not . . . I only wanted . . ."

"Doesn't matter," Grayson said with a finality that shut Ace up and pulled his chest tight.

Otis let them off on a floor that, for once, didn't look exciting or cutting edge or made to delight the eleven-to-thirteen-year-old crowd. In fact, it looked like a regular office floor in some boring skyscraper. Only it was dim, and everyone who worked there was probably asleep.

Gray led the way to a large corner office. He flung the door open and sat in the chair in front of the large desk. He kicked his legs over the arm of the chair and let his head dangle back.

Ace decided that silence was going to be his best defense, even if it felt impossible. Leo rolled over and collapsed their face into their hands.

"I'm sorry," Ace whispered to his new boxmates. "I just thought if—"

"It's my fault. I shouldn't have brought you up there."

"You really shouldn't have, Grayson. You have those codes for *emergencies,* not for fooling around," a deep, oddly familiar voice said, making Ace straighten up. One second they were alone, and the next, a holographic image flicked into place, and Dr. Lance Bix was scowling hard at his son, seated at the desk. He was tall and so lean, with dark skin and buzzed hair that turned silver on the sides.

Ace had seen so many videos of Dr. Bix on the B.E.S.T. website and in interviews about the discovery of Bixonium, but he hadn't seen this side of the legendary scientist.

The dad side.

Dr. Bix cleared his throat. "I'd say that I'm disappointed in you, but mostly I'm surprised. After our last chat, and considering the arrangement *you* insisted on, I assumed you'd be on the straight and narrow for your remaining time at ToP."

"Dad, I didn't—"

"You act as if you're invisible, Grayson. You are the opposite. Everyone has noticed that you haven't taken up an aptitude for or even an interest in any one aug, and you are three months from your thirteenth birthday, young man."

Ace moved forward, twisting out of Leo's grip on his wrist. "It's my fault, Dr. Bix," he said, shrinking when Dr. Bix's surprisingly strong holographic stare hit him. "I'm new, sir. And I was upset that I had to wait until second semester to see the Coliseum." Ace had a flash of his earlier frustration. "Because, really? That's what we're all here for, sir, why would you tease us like that? Also it's my birthday, sir, and Gray wanted to do something nice."

Dr. Bix seemed shocked by Ace's runaway mouth. This was not that unusual for Ace, so he kept going. "We were just going to look around, but I got so excited, and I've been dreaming about SuperSoar since I first got my SAR deck." Ace instinctively pulled out the card he kept in his pocket. Dr. Bix glanced down at it. "I shouldn't have climbed that tower. It's all my fault. I could have gotten in more than trouble. I could have died."

The last word struck Dr. Bix's holographic image. He paused for a moment as if he needed to reorder his thoughts, and when he spoke again, some of the Disappointed Dad tone was gone. "No one has ever died at ToP. And no one ever will. But your actions were dangerous. You'll be calling home and letting your parents know that you're one day in and one strike down. What's your name?"

"Ace Wells."

Another pause. And Ace *knew* what was coming next.

"Finnegan's little brother?"

"Yes, sir."

"I was on the phone with your family earlier this evening. To thank your brother for services to his country. Your brother's actions have been invaluable." Dr. Bix's holograph flickered as he leaned back in his chair. He linked his long hands and looped them behind his head. "But I'd like to expect even more from you, Ace."

"Really?" Ace's whole body was surprised. "Me too, sir. To be honest."

"I won't be uttering the words *strike two* with you, will I? Good." Dr. Bix actually laughed—before he stopped abruptly. "Now, Leo. This is strike two, isn't it?"

"Don't punish Leo. They didn't do anything!" Gray stood, valiantly getting in the way of Dr. Bix's view of his best friend.

"You should've thought of that before you roped them in." Bix swiped a hand toward his son, and Gray sat down hard. "Leo, you're benched for the first three games of the season. I'll let Coach Hernandez know."

"*Three?*" Leo seemed like they'd shrunk, collapsing with disappointment.

"Ace and Leo, you two take off. My son and I have to adjust our arrangement, since our compromise clearly isn't working for him."

Gray's shoulders slumped further, which didn't even feel possible. Leo tugged Ace's shirt and wheeled out. Ace followed.

They were back in Otis before Ace cleared his throat. "Do you think Gray will be in real trouble? I don't have a dad. He seemed kind of . . . intense."

Leo took off their glasses and rubbed the lenses on their shirt. "Dr. Bix isn't intense. He loves his son an awful lot. And he *really* loves for his son to do as he's told. And not cause waves like his mom."

"What happened with his mom?"

"I shouldn't have said that. Forget it." Leo replaced their glasses.

The silence was killer. "I'm sorry you won't be able to play in your games."

Leo didn't say anything.

The elevator doors opened on their floor, but before they could enter their box, Leo spun in a circle to face Ace. "I don't know what you're after, but Gray isn't some celebrity you can glom onto. He's got his own goals, and what you did tonight probably ruined the deal he made with his dad."

"Deal?"

"To pick his own aug. Gray should have had his implant last semester, but he couldn't decide, and Dr. Bix said he could have more time to think about how he wants to be augmented. Thing is, Gray isn't sure he wants to get augmented."

"What?! But that's—"

"Not possible for the only son of the inventor of augs." Leo's look was piercing. "Is it?"

Ace shook his head. "And I thought I had problems."

"You do have problems, Ace. Number one? Your box-mates can't trust you." Leo entered the box with a sharp pivot. Jayla was nowhere to be seen, and Ace found himself alone in the common room, waiting for Gray to come back so that he could say he was so sorry. Make it up to him. Do *something*.

Gray didn't come back, and Ace spent his first night at the Tower of Power on a bed that couldn't hold on to its sheets.

◙

By the time dawn cracked across the sky and filled Ace's window with an orangey-purple light, Ace dialed home on his tablet. Mom would be up; Mama Jay and Finn shouldn't be.

"My baby!" Mom said as she answered the video call, hair a mess but smile bright. "What are you doing up so early? How was your first day? Have you blown them all away?" She paused to examine his face. "Baby? Something wrong? Are you worried about Finn? Because he's perfectly fine. Better than fine! You should see what Dr. Bix sent him as a present."

Ace didn't have to answer. His face folded up, and Mom's expression quieted. She waited for him to speak. "It's not Finn. I got in trouble . . . already. I'm supposed to let you know."

"You okay?"

Ace nodded, but the up and down of his head turned into a side-to-side *no*. "I was thinking about getting my wings, and I wasn't thinking about my boxmates, and I got them in trouble, and I feel really, *really* bad. This was supposed to be my place to shine, to really be me, and now it feels like school all over again, with no one wanting to hang out with me and teachers thinking I can't follow directions." His voice broke. "This was going to be my place."

Mom didn't say anything for a moment. "Hard to walk around inside a dream, isn't it?"

"Yeah."

He sniffed.

"Yeah." Mom always understood. "Being awake is the hardest part of following your dreams, love. It won't be like you've always imagined. It'll be messier and greater and so much harder. You might have to make some new goals. Change your plans."

Ace nodded, and she said some more mushy things that made him feel better but also worry if his boxmates could hear through the walls.

By the time he hung up, he felt like he'd taken one

huge step onto the other side of something. He needed a new plan. One that would make him less like Finn 2.0, the person who played heroics for attention and made fans instead of friends.

Ace made a new vow to be there for his boxmates. He'd be a friend—a real one. The next time his boxmates had a little dinner party with fried rice and dumplings, he'd be right there with them, laughing, listening to music, a part of their team. He'd wait patiently for his aug like everyone else. No more Bix fanboy.

Ace threw his SAR deck in the trash.

LEVEL TWO:

BE A FRIEND

8

GillGraft

Aug Track: Boost
Breathe underwater.

Four weeks later, Ace dangled upside down from a trapeze bar. All the blood had long ago rushed into his face, and he was straining to keep his muscles tight and knees hooked over the bar.

"Looks like he's trying to take a dump!" Siff called out from below, treading water in the deep pool beneath the trapeze equipment.

"Ewww," the circle of first semester cadets around Siff all chorused. His cadet pack had just recently moved from the safety procedures of level one (snooze) to trying out all the wild equipment in level two, which came in the form of somewhat familiar challenges.

Of course, Ace now felt stupid about having been extra excited when Vaughn told the cadet pack they were going to play sharks and minnows, which was supposed to demonstrate leadership and daring. Ace had played this game at his old school, and he was so tiny and fast that it was one of the games he wasn't bad at, running from one side of the gym to the other, diving around the bigger kids, the sharks, who by tagging turned you into a shark, as if this state were a communicable disease.

But then Ace found out that sharks and minnows at B.E.S.T. meant the minnows flew on trapezes until they fell into the sea-green pool below, where the "sharks" were waiting. When Siff had volunteered to be the first shark, Ace's worries tripled. Particularly when Siff's "tags" were more like aggressive dunkings that left the new shark sputtering water in the aftermath.

Now Ace was the sole minnow left, dangling only a few feet above two dozen chanting, jeering sharks, who seemed to be excitedly proving that bullying was also contagious. He swung so that he could at least get a hand on the bar. This took a little pressure off his knees, but he would be falling at some point. It was only a matter of time.

The doomsday clock of the day.

Somewhere above, on the catwalk over the trapeze swings, Vaughn hollered, "The sharks are circling, Wells! Make a move."

Ace managed to pull his stomach tight enough to swing up, grabbing the thick wires that held the bar, wobbling wildly. The sharks below groaned as they treaded water.

Carlos, the aug assist, was sitting on the trapeze opposite him, legs impossibly wound around the bar, showing off his flexibility aug. "You're pretty dead. Might as well fall."

"Maybe I'm waiting for the sharks to drown."

"Vaughn will have Amir mess with the bars before that. Believe me, you'd rather fall of your own accor—Oh, too late."

Ace clearly hadn't moved fast enough, and now his trapeze was lowering toward the surface of the pool a few inches at a time. The sharks hollered with psychotic delight, their "food" coming straight to them. Ace panicked, standing up on the bar, wobbling all over. Carlos was right; better to go down because he made a stupid choice than have a stupid choice made for him.

Ace dived in the opposite direction of the circling sharks.

He hit the water with a hard splash and instantly felt the chaos of dozens of cadets swimming at him. He had one choice. Ace had close to zero body fat, which was only good for sinking. This had become a patented move to get away from Finn, who often seemed like he had been born with an invisible shark fin.

Ace let out all of his breath and felt himself dropping away from the rest of the kicking, thrashing bodies. How deep was this pool anyway?

Answer: deeper than he'd thought.

When he'd used this technique with Finn, Ace always had just enough breath to hit the bottom and kick back up to the surface in a different direction.

Not this time.

Ace's lungs started to pulse with the urge to breathe, *breathe*. If he had the GillGraft aug, he'd just inhale this water, his lungs pulling the oxygen out of the H_2O. It took all of his energy to keep his mouth shut and his nose pinched. He cracked his eyes open and looked around for some kind of help. All he saw were legs high, high above. Little legs and tiny feet.

With a pop of black across his vision, he couldn't stop his body a second longer.

He breathed in all the water at once.

A minute later he was puking by the side of the pool, next to a wet and aggravated Carlos. Vaughn slapped his back while the sharks — who Ace couldn't even think of as cadets anymore — made grossed-out sounds with each blue-green water retch and cough.

"Let's make a lesson out of Wells, shall we?" Vaughn said, not unkindly, but not kind at all considering he'd just nearly drowned. "Your plans for winning should never surpass your plans for surviving."

Siff barked a laugh, but Vaughn scowled. "I'm serious, Malone. Class dismissed."

The cadets took off, and Ace tried to stand. Coach Vaughn put a hand on his shoulder and pushed him back down. "You've got to head to 101 and get checked out by a nurse before you rejoin your classmates."

"Guessed as much." Ace knew enough about ToP now to know that 101 was the med level. The nurse's office and more. His head hung low, his eyes tracing the brilliant Bixonics green of the tile around the pool.

Wild screams leaked out from the direction of the locker room.

"Make sure they're behaving," Vaughn said to the aug assistants. Ace watched Carlos, Alexandra, and Amir head off to the locker room.

Alone with the teacher . . . Ace knew this feeling too well. It fell on top of him like a blanket. Not a warm, comforting kind, but the smothering of Finn pinning Ace beneath his own comforter while Ace yowled like a cat in a bag.

"You're going to tell me I have to change my ways or I'm out." Ace's throat hurt from coughing up salty water.

"No." Vaughn's tone was soft. "You'd have to cheat in some way or harm someone to get kicked out. Accidentally harming yourself out of sheer will to win isn't currently in the code of conduct. Although if we have to add it, we can call it the Ace Rule."

Ace didn't laugh, but it was a little funny.

Vaughn sighed. "I was going to ask how you've made it this far when your mortality doesn't rank that high on your priorities."

"Honestly?" Ace shrugged. "No idea."

"You've been here nearly a month now, and I've watched you risk your life twice. I thought at first that you might be the bad kind of trouble, but I think it's worse. You're what happens when bad trouble has a good heart." Ace looked up at his coach. Or was Vaughn his teacher? Both, maybe. "This happen a lot to you before you came here?" Vaughn asked.

"This?"

"Trial by pubescent sharks."

Ace wanted to lie; he couldn't. "My principal used to say that it was like I had a big neon sign over my head that read 'Pick on me.'"

"Sounds like a bad principal." Vaughn grunted. "You know you won, Wells?"

"I did?"

"You were the last minnow. No one tagged you."

"Yay," Ace squeaked weakly.

Vaughn helped Ace to his feet with a firm hand on his elbow. "Look, I know you want to be alone . . ." Ace had a weird feeling as he processed those words. He *did* want to be alone. How did Vaughn know? "But get checked out with the nurse first, Wells. And then maybe work on that standoff with Malone before you two ruin each other's chances at a promising future."

"Thanks for the advice, sir." Ace wrapped a fluffy towel around himself and walked toward the elevators.

He pressed the button, dripping on the floor. The elevator didn't come, not for long minutes, and Ace started to shiver, his lips bouncing off each other. Finally, a loud group of cadets sounded in the hall from behind, and Ace hit the button again. "Come on, Otis!" he whispered. "They'll eat me for real this time."

The elevator appeared just as the cadets reached him, and they all piled into the car together. Ace pulled his towel more tightly just as Siff's taunting voice filled the small space. "The drowned rat, Ace the drudge. Making every challenge last twice as long."

Ace spun around and shot his hand out toward Siff, to shake. "Good game, shark!" he said boldly despite his chattering teeth. "That was apex, wasn't it?"

Siff looked down at Ace's pruned fingers. "I don't shake hands. It's antiquated."

Ace had to thank Mom's huge vocabulary for helping him with this one; Siff had clearly used this fancy word for "old-fashioned" to stump him. He dropped his hand, but he wasn't backing down. "It's antiquated to be a good sport?"

Siff's blue eyes narrowed on Ace, his blond hair nearly black when it was wet and combed back tightly against his head. "Yes."

Ace laughed suddenly — because that had to be a joke — surprising the cadets in the elevator, who peered over Siff's shoulder, watching this exchange with unblinking eyes.

"Why are you *laughing?*" Siff snapped, pinching his head like he had a headache.

"Because I thought life at ToP was going to be, like, the best, if you can handle the pun. So much better than public school, where being mean was some sort of status. But then you come around, all nasty for no reason, and remind me that *real* drudges are everywhere."

To be fair, Ace hadn't meant to call Siff a drudge.

That had just *happened.*

And he regretted it the second that the cadets cheered at his insult, and Siff's face folded with anger.

"Open the doors, idiot elevator! We're *hungry,*" Siff hollered.

As if the AI was also afraid of Siff, Otis opened the doors to the cafeteria so fast that two feet of the floor below was showing. The cadets climbed out of the elevator — literally — while Ace watched them go, wanting to say something. To take back his insult. To do something differently. He wasn't the person who called people names. Not even at the people who called him names.

Ace had been working on his plan to make friends for almost a month.

And so far he was pretty sure he'd only made things worse.

"Sorry," Ace said quietly when Siff was the last to leave.

Siff held the door with one hand and glared back at Ace. "I'm not trying to be your enemy or bully. I'm trying to win. To be head of our cadet pack. Demonstrated leaders always get tracked for Brain. And I *have to* get tracked for Brain. So stop being a complete baby and making all this so personal."

Siff climbed out and the doors shut, and the elevator felt weirdly paused.

"Level 101, Otis. I have to see the nurse before I'm cleared to return to my schedule."

The elevator began to lower, slowly, steadily. Ace took the opportunity to sit on the ground in his towel and put his head in hands.

"Your vitals are stable, and yet your posture indicates frailty," Otis said.

"You ever want to do something? *One* thing? And everything you try makes that one thing more impossible?"

"I've never wanted anything," Otis said. "To want is rather human, not easily mapped by artificial intelligence. To give software a motivation is a dangerous process. I am programmed for independent thought and behavior, but not to desire outcomes."

"You're lucky. Wanting things is probably the worst part of being human."

Ace tried not to think about how Finn kept calling him, probably because he *knew* Ace was blowing it, but he wouldn't give Finn the satisfaction of rubbing it in. Ace had thirteen missed calls from his big brother. Sometimes he felt sort of proud of that fact. Other times he was just plain nervous. What if Finn showed up here?

"What might your parental unit advise on the subject?" Otis asked.

"My parents? I *do not* want them to know how much I'm blowing this. They already know I got in trouble the first day. They don't need to hear that the longest conversation I've had since coming here was with my aug coach and the misfit elevator."

"Misfit." Otis paused. "Meaning a conspicuous being whose behavior creates discomfort among others. Am I truly *misfit,* Ace Wells?"

"You are. But it's not a bad thing. It just means you're doing your own thing." The doors opened, and Ace stepped out. "Thanks, Otis."

"You're welcome, Ace Wells."

XConnect

Aug Track: Brain
You are one with technology.

Jayla was in the common room when Ace got back to Lilliput. He wasn't wet anymore, but he was wearing hospital scrubs, since the nurse didn't want him walking back to his box in his bathing suit.

Jayla hooked one eyebrow when he entered, taking in his outfit. "Hanging out at 101?"

"Nearly drowned. I'm fine."

"Oh, *nearly?* Nearly makes it all right." She laughed that good laugh. The one that made Ace feel less alone. Leo and Gray had spent the last few weeks dodging him; they were so exceptional at it that Ace was starting to think they knew about secret tunnels in this skyscraper or something. Jayla *had* been around, although she was always playing with her new aug. Ace swore she hadn't looked up from the interface on her forearm since her surgery over a month ago. He hadn't gotten close enough to see the interface in action yet, but he was dying to.

Was it like a tablet screen? Or something more? The distant look he'd stolen at Amir's interface hadn't made sense to him, but then, Amir's first language was Arabic.

Jayla looked stellar as ever. She wore red boots that went all the way to her knees, a denim romper, and that berry-blue lipstick that was definitely part of her signature look. Ace had been learning things about Jayla for a while now, since she didn't seem to mind him hanging around. Twice a week, her group of BFFs came over to write songs. Band name: the ToP Beatz.

"Newk, it's creepy to watch people." Jayla didn't look up. "Even with your peripherals."

Busted. "Sorry."

Jayla put her arm down and cocked her head. "What's the deal though, really? I checked out of box life for one night to get ready for my aug implant, and when I get back everyone is peeved at you. When I asked Leo, they said you couldn't be trusted. Which, ouch."

"Yeah, I screwed up bad." Ace sat in the pod chair that spun in a pleasing circle. "But when did you ask them that? Recently?"

"A few days ago."

That was the true *ouch*. Ace hadn't been able to prove his loyalty to either of his other two boxmates for weeks now. Probably because they were so dynamite at dodging him.

"So they're not close to forgiving me." Ace's heart felt like someone stepped on it for a hot second. "Any advice for getting back in their good graces?"

"Time and space. Lots of it." Jayla picked up her arm again and dragged one finger down the white screen beneath her illuminated brown skin. Ace knew that her arm was like a remote, helping her control all the new abilities in her augged-up brain, but he was desperate to ask questions. He sat on them instead. Well, he sat on his hands. It didn't help. Then he spun so fast in the pod chair that the world went blurry.

Leo wheeled out of their room on their smaller sports chair, wearing their BESTBall jersey. After a quick nod at Jayla and a glance at a now dizzy Ace, they went to Grayson's room and knocked. Grayson opened the door, wearing black sunglasses with very black lenses.

"Oh, yes!" Jayla cheered. "VisionX simulators. How are you liking them?"

Grayson shrugged. Did he just look at Ace? Did Ace's face just light up like a stoplight? What did *that* look like through the VisionX simulator glasses? The aug could help you zoom in, zoom out, map infrared images, and even see in the dark.

"I like them fine." Gray's voice seemed to disagree. "Well, not all the time."

Leo leaned forward on their knees, chin propped on their palm. "Gray has to try out a new aug simulator every two weeks until he picks. Dad's orders. He's only got three more months before his thirteenth birthday."

Gray shook his head as if warding off those words. Ace was surprised to realize that he was more than nervous about getting an aug. Maybe even scared. Why?

Ace spoke up before he could think better of it. "But you should be psyched to get your aug. The whole world can't wait to hear what you pick!"

Gray winced; Leo shot him a warning look. "Great, thanks for reminding me. Emma has been updating her feed with every aug I try out, doing status reports on me. Which means a host of her followers are signing out the same trial augs. My own personal army of drudgy wannabe clones." He adjusted the glasses. "I just wish there was a way to turn off the stupid trial aug for an hour. This is the best one I've tried so far, but I just want to go back to normal for the game. Last thing I want is to accidentally watch the infrared highlights of the players' sweat spots."

Leo chuckled, but when Ace joined in, they held up one stiff finger to cut him off.

Clearly he was still in the penalty box.

"A tech need, you say?" Jayla jumped up as if someone was offering her an ice cream buffet. "Yes, yes, yes. Let me try!"

She got right in front of Grayson and touched the side

of the glasses. "Link established," she narrated, biting her lower lip, clearly delighted by this challenge. "*Pause operations for one hour.* There. That should work."

Gray took the glasses off and turned them around in his hand. "Wow, they're just sunglasses now. Are you sure my coach won't be able to tell?"

"She'll know they went offline, but not why. I spent my first week with XConnect building elaborate security screens to mask every single thing I do."

"Course you did." Gray bumped fists with Jayla. "BIPOC meeting Friday."

"Already on the calendar," Jayla said.

"Thanks." He turned to Leo. "Ready?"

"Am I ready to watch my team struggle from the bench, unable to do anything?" they asked, eyes darting toward Ace. "Sure."

Leo and Grayson left, and Jayla sat back on the couch next to Ace. She whistled one long, ominous note. "So maybe more than time and space to get back in L's and G's good graces. Maybe chocolate and chores and begging and penance."

"Should I meet this Emma? Tell her to back off?"

She barked a short laugh. "What? No! Emma's a subject you shouldn't go anywhere near."

Ace clapped two hands over his face. "How can I be so bad at being human? Is there an aug for that one yet? It could be called like SocialPlus, or something."

Jayla laughed. "You are funny, little newk. But mostly the laughing is at you, not with you. You might want to work on that."

"That's exactly what I've been doing since I got here. Or at least I thought I was," Ace deadpanned. A blister was on the verge of breaking open on his palm, a leftover reminder from gripping the trapeze bar with all his might. He shouldn't poke at it. He poked at it. "I don't get this. Any of it. We do these challenges with our cadet pack, but it doesn't seem to matter who wins."

"You've got Vaughn, right?" Ace nodded, and Jayla continued. "He doesn't care who wins what. The outcome is secondary to the actions you take to get there. He's watching all of you, trying to decide if you should be placed on the Brain, Bod, or Boost track."

"I want to be Bod. I have to be Bod."

"Famous last words of someone assigned to Boost." One of those perfect eyebrows arched again. "When are you scheduled in the ER?"

"Emergency room?!"

"Escape room. End of level two, before you get sorted into your aug category. Or get held back."

There it was.

More proof that Ace really could easily get knocked off-track at B.E.S.T. He'd been obsessively worried about getting kicked out — but getting held back would also be terrible. Finn would never let him live it down.

In all his years of research, he'd never read anything about an escape room on the Bixonics website. Everyone always succeeded in the testimonials. Everyone always received the aug they yearned for. He thought about SuperSoar and felt his spirits do the opposite of soar. What even was that? Nosedive? He sank so far into the pod chair that he worried about getting stuck there.

Jayla went back to her arm, and Ace watched for a long minute. "You're staring again."

"Sorry." Ace grabbed a tube of yogurt from the small fridge and went to his room to change. He didn't even get his shoes off before he screamed the wildest scream of his short, un-augged life.

Jayla came running in, kicking the door open with those amazing boots, arms in a locked position as if she'd spent some time studying martial arts. "What's wrong?"

Ace stood there holding the scrubs over his chest. He nodded toward the corner of the room, where the Finn-yata sat on his desk chair. Finn's tissue-box head was half off the shoebox shoulders, but the black eyes were staring and the smile was oh so creepy.

"What in the wide world of bots is that?" Jayla yelled, arms dropping but voice rising.

"A sign that my brother has been here. Have you seen him?"

"Your brother Finn was here? In our box? When?"

"I don't know, but he obviously left that for me to find."

"You got family issues, newk." Jayla shook her head.

Ace threw a towel over the demented piñata. "He must be mad that I've been dodging his calls. He keeps tabs on me." Ace was shaking a bit. This was a lot, even for Finn.

Jayla stepped closer and peered into his eyes. "You okay?" Ace nodded unconvincingly, and she exhaled for a long moment. "So, I have to go try out the new simulation software I'm writing. I'm probably going to regret this, but do you want to come? I need a guinea pig."

Ace's joy blasted out of him. "Do I!"

Jayla cringed. "Yeah, some advice. Don't be too excited to sign up for the utterly unknown at ToP." She scooped up the Finn-yata inside the towel. "And let's drop this off in the chute for the trash compactor on the way."

◧

An hour later, Ace found himself in a place he hadn't been yet. It was a level full of little white cubicles with lids. Jayla tucked into the first vacant one and tossed her jacket in the corner. "Sit."

"Where?" he asked.

"In the middle. On the floor."

Ace did as he was told, watching as Jayla touched her hand to the side of the white cubicle until a tone sounded, indicating that a link had been established. "What's this simulation software supposed to do?"

"What it's always supposed to do. Trick your brain into thinking it's real." Jayla concentrated as she called up colorful lights and buttons on her forearm. A control pad that could possibly be used to control *anything*.

"How does your aug work?" Ace asked, fascinated. "Does it turn your body into a computer?"

Jayla paused. "My brain is the computer, but my body is being used as a huge battery. As long as I'm in good health, I can do just about anything I want with it. It takes time. And skill. Some super-skilled people with XConnect don't need the interface after a few years. They can do it all in their head. That will be me."

"Like long division." Ace had a teacher once who'd tried to get him to *envision the numbers,* since patience for writing them out was too hard. Guess what? The patience to envision them was also beyond his ability.

She pressed something hard on her arm, and all of a sudden the white cubicle flashed Bixonics green.

"We're in the ToP mainframe now," Jayla muttered.

"Cool."

"Not cool. I was trying to get us out of it." Jayla did some more fancy finger work on her forearm and the green walls and floor slowly, surely, turned as berry blue as Jayla's lips. Jayla did a little dance to celebrate her success and shut the door, sealing them in the cool blue light.

"Where are we now?" Ace asked, enchanted by the soft, beautiful glow.

"We're in the Brain pod room."

"You know what I mean." Ace walked around the space, taking in the way the light was seamless. A dream within a dream.

"We're in *my* mainframe. It's small and new, but it exists entirely outside of ToP security."

"What can we do here?"

"Anything you want, for the most part." Jayla was grinning at Ace's entranced expression. "Like *this*."

Jayla called up an image of Coach Vaughn. It was so lifelike that Ace laughed and shoved a hand right through his coach's hologram chest. *Weird.*

"If you don't touch it, it'll seem more real. Go ahead, ask him to put you in Bod."

Ace didn't wait. "Bod track, Vaughn! On the double." Okay, that was too saucy even for Ace. "Please?"

Hologram Vaughn smiled and held out a red wristband. It magically transferred from his coach's hand to Ace's wrist. Ace turned his arm over and over. Red for Bod track. So much closer to SuperSoar than he'd let himself dream recently. He grinned at Jayla. "What else can it do?"

"Well, the simulation is limited because this is mostly designed to become its own communication outlink. A way to talk to people outside of ToP without Bixonics knowing."

"Why would you need that?"

"Why *wouldn't* you?" Jayla squinted at him. "Do you have any idea how intrusive the Bixonics security measures are? Each minute you're here is on file in the database. *Tracked.*" Ace blinked at her, and she shrugged. "Okay, you want to call someone?"

"Like my parents? Yeah!"

"Call Ace's family home." Jayla had such pride in her voice as she commanded her own network.

The little box full of blueberry light ebbed softly, and suddenly, a lifelike, full-size simulation of Mama Jay appeared in the pod, wearing her lifting gear and a light sweat. "Whatever you're selling, we're not buying." She rested her large body on one of the kitchen stools.

"Mama Jay!" Ace yelled, not prepared for the bright tears that popped into his eyes. "It's me, your Ace!"

"Acey, love! What are you doing calling on a blocked number? You're lucky I answered. Mom would have sent it to videomail."

"My boxmate Jayla has the XConnect aug, and she made this amazing communication software that can also simulate people, and I can see you like you're in this space with me. Can you see me?"

"Only on the wall screen. You look good, a little blue. Not like sad, more like . . . actually blue?"

"That's Jayla's signature color."

Jayla laughed into the back of her hand.

Ace remembered the haunting gift he'd found in his box earlier. "Do you know what Finn was doing at ToP today?"

"Finn ran over to ToP today?" Mama Jay asked, the words slow and full of aggravation. "That's news to me."

Ohhh, Finn was in trouble now. Apex.

Ace walked as close to the simulation of Mama Jay as he could. He wanted to reach for her, but Jayla was right. It would feel more real if he didn't try to touch her. "I miss you," he blurted. He didn't even care if Jayla heard him. "It's really hard to get to know people. *Really* hard. No one likes me."

"Kid, that's not true. Can't be." Mama Jay started to say something but then shook her head as if changing her mind. "Find the people who make you feel safe enough to be yourself. The rest is easy."

Well, now what did that mean?

"Feel the fear and do it anyway, Acey."

Jayla waved a finger around to signal that he should wrap it up. Ace bid Mama Jay farewell with instructions for her to hug Mom from him — which she agreed to do — and put Ace's fake-but-so-realistic snake in Finn's bed — which she said she'd think about doing, especially after he'd run two states away without permission.

By the time Ace hung up, Jayla was sitting on the floor. Looking . . . strange. Tired, maybe.

"Are you okay? Did I zap your human battery too much?"

"Nah, it would take a lot more to drain me." She sighed. "You really think no one likes you? Is this just because L and G are holding a grudge?"

"My pack isn't a big fan of me. There's a bully involved. It's all rather stereotypical, if you ask me."

Jayla chuckled. Ace sat next to her, shoulder to shoulder. Did he feel safe enough to be himself around Jayla? Maybe? A little? He was usually so busy being intimidated by her that he wasn't sure about the rest of it.

"Your mom is pretty dynamite, you know that?"

"She can bench-press 250. That's almost three of me."

Jayla closed her eyes and let her head slip back. She didn't move for a long second. "I miss my family too. I don't get to go home for break between semesters like everyone else."

"Why?"

"For my reasons. Personal ones." Her voice was hard and flat, but then it got soft. "I miss my daddy so much. We have like an entire language of inside jokes."

Ace felt overwhelmed by the need to do something nice for her. He'd been all slouchy when they came in, and now he felt powered up by having seen Mama Jay—and ratting out Finn.

"Call Jayla's dad," he told the blue cubicle.

The box around them turned even more blue, deeper blue, and Jayla jumped to her feet. She seemed stunned at first, and Ace saw the ocean all around, cobalt and endless.

He heard it too. Oceans and gulls and—was that the symbol for a tree? The image was overlaid like a watermark, but it was also familiar. The branches as numerous as the roots . . .

"Cancel! Cancel the call now!" Jayla yelled as she found her voice.

The ocean and tree disappeared as fast as it had appeared. Jayla's fingers desperately worked over her forearm, and the pod washed Bixonics green and then back to all white.

"I've seen that tree before! It was on those protesters' signs out front of the B.E.S.T. enrollment office. What's it supposed to mean?"

Jayla turned to Ace. She was so wildly upset that he was suddenly scared he'd done something super wrong. "How could you do that? What's *wrong* with you?"

"I was trying to help you! Like you helped me."

"You have no idea what you've done! Ugh, I have so much scrubbing to do . . . This is bad."

"I'm sorry!" Ace squeaked.

Jayla scowled and pointed to the exit. "Go away, Ace."

10

PassPort

Aug Track: Brain
Speak any language. Master communication.

"Then she was like, *go away*," Ace recounted in the elevator.

It had been a week after his incident with Jayla and each day he wished he'd start to feel less bad about how he'd blown it with her. Today wasn't that day, which was why he'd sought out the (surprisingly) best ear at ToP: Otis. Although he was careful to leave out the details about Jayla's family that felt . . . mysterious. Just in case.

Ace continued after a sigh. "It felt like she was saying, *get out of my life forever*. Like the way Leo and Grayson are just done with me. Worst part is, I don't blame them. I got Gray in trouble with his dad, and I got Leo benched, and Jayla had to do a lot of *scrubbing* . . . whatever that means."

"Scrubbing is often used to describe the process of deleting stored information in a database," Otis offered. "And then deleting the record of the deletion."

Ace sat hard on the floor of the elevator car, staring out the glass wall at the sky full of neon clouds that would one day be home to people with SuperSoar, and those people might not include Ace after all because everything he wanted crashed in his hands. "What do you know about cadets failing out of B.E.S.T.? Everyone keeps hinting at it, but no one says anything real."

"I know everything about everyone," Otis answered.

"See? That's one of those lines you've got to work on. It's creepy." Ace sat up, facing the screen of the control board, which he'd taught Otis to outfit with something like a face, numbers lit up like two eyes, a nose, and mouth. "Maybe next time say something like, 'Sure, I know about failing out. Here's some information.'"

"Sure, I know about failing out. Here's some information."

Ace waited, but Otis was done, literal to the smallest detail. "Yeah, but after you say it, you have to give the person the information."

"People aren't good at information. They curate, pick and choose, forget facts in favor of a specific narrative." Otis paused. "For example, if I told you that fifteen percent of all first semester cadets fail level two instead of getting tracked, you would decide that you must be in that percentage and doom yourself to further failure."

"Fifteen percent!" Ace yelled.

"You are proving my point."

The elevator doors dinged and opened before Ace was ready. He didn't scramble to his feet fast enough, and Leo rolled in on their red sports chair, one eyebrow raised and uniform on. "What are you doing in here?" they asked.

"I'm . . . just . . ."

"I have become Ace Wells's only friend. Ace Wells is my only friend, too," Otis recounted. "We are made for each—"

"Okay, Otis, let's get Leo to their game!" Ace said loudly over Otis's embarrassing declaration. The doors closed, and the car dropped while Leo watched Ace.

Watched him hard.

When the elevator dinged for the stadium level, Leo rolled halfway out and stopped. "Come with me, Ace."

Ace thought this might be a trick, but he jumped to follow, leaving Otis behind with a quick fist bump on the control panel.

"Where are we going?" he asked after a minute.

"I get to play today. Finally. I figure if my punishment is over, yours should wrap up too."

Ace didn't exactly know what that meant, but it sounded . . . good? Maybe? "We could be friends," he found himself saying before he'd approved the words in his head.

Leo's answer was that patented silence.

The stadium around the court wasn't crowded quite yet. Ace was early, arriving at the same time as the players. He watched Leo speed out into the middle of the court, snag the neon ball, and wheel hard and fast toward one end zone. The rest of their teammates jumped to catch up, but none could. They were *fast,* but it was more than speed, almost like the sport put them in their best headspace. Mama Jay always said something similar about lifting weights, that it made her brain happy.

Ace looked for a place to sit in the stands, which were just starting to fill with cadets. He saw Grayson—who quickly looked the other way—and Ace realized that whatever pass Leo was ready to give him, Gray wasn't there yet. Ace sat alone, off to the side, waiting for the players to finish warm-up and for the game to begin.

"Hey! You're Ace Wells!"

Ace looked up to find a pretty, familiar person staring at him.

Emma.

"Yeah, I'm Ace."

"Excellent!" Emma hugged him. "That's from Finn."

Ace blinked one eye at a time.

"I'm Emma, semester two, she/her. You probably know me from my news feed." She smiled and sat next to him.

So this was the infamous Emma in person! Ace couldn't help but be intrigued; he hadn't told any of his boxmates, but he had been watching all her news vids. Well, he didn't have much else to do. "Your brother thinks you might need a friend, and so he messaged me. We DM."

Ace cocked his head way back to look at Emma. Without the filters and lights and makeup, she looked *a lot* like Leo. Dark hair, pale white skin, piercing eyes. "I'm pretty sure that if you talked to my brother, he wouldn't tell you to hug me."

"Fine, he told me to throw you in a headlock and rough up your hair. I *translated* that to mean brotherly affection, and therefore a hug. I'm on track for PassPort," she added, as if she could not stop herself. She held out her hand to show off her blue-for-Brain wristband.

PassPort was the aug for learning languages, becoming an expert in communication, one of the prized Brain augs that Ace had honestly sort of skipped over most of the time. Even in SAR, the card didn't have a lot of draw.

"Ah, great. You're Leo's sister, right?"

Emma's intense frown creased her face. "Did Leo not tell you they have a twin?"

"No." Emma was Leo's *twin?* Whoa. That was a weird

secret to be sitting on. "But to be honest, Leo has said about seven things to me since I moved in."

"That scans," Emma confirmed with a clipped tone. "I am the talker in the family."

The stadium was filled up now, and they had to scoot closer to each other on the bench as it was getting crowded. A lot of cadets were wearing jerseys for either the second semester team, Leo's team, or their opponents, the third semester team. He saw two people wearing Leo's number, and he had the oddest little buzz of pride. That was *his* boxmate. Sure, Leo wasn't crazy about Ace at the moment, but maybe that could change. He was already doing okay with Emma; that had to be good news.

Emma was also looking over the audience, eyes snagging on Leo's fans, although she didn't seem as happy about this as Ace was.

"So, you're already on track for a specific aug?" Ace asked, trying to start a new conversation. "I thought you were supposed to have just your track by second semester."

"Some people are more decided than others. Like your boxmate Jayla," Emma said. Ace's whole body sank at Jayla's name. Guilt squirmed, but also confusion and regret. "She always knew she wanted XConnect, and that's why she's at the front of the third semester cadet pack. The first one to get her aug implant."

Emma kept talking as if they were instant best friends, and Ace's suspicion started to grow, remembering Jayla's warning about Leo's sibling. "I think it's Grayson's influence, honestly. Leo should have had their aug category picked out by now. We're already over one-third of the way through the semester."

"But Leo is tracked for all three. Isn't that beyond awesome?" Ace wondered if Emma could hear the jealousy in his voice.

"They're cleared for all three tracks, sure, but they have to choose ASAP. And they aren't choosing. They're browsing. It's maddening, and they're probably doing it just to make me annoyed. Leo's always doing, never thinking. Never deciding."

Oof, okay. That was a nerve. Ace quickly changed the subject. "I don't know enough about BESTBall. Did it start at ToP?"

Ace had done a good job; Emma started talking like a tour guide, waving her hand as she described how the game worked, where it came from, etc. Ace learned that BESTBall had been invented in 2038 by aug athlete Darren Sue Francis. The sport combined the aggressive nature and field tactics of something called *rugby* with an interactive court. Ten players in wheelchairs fielded the court, five per team, working together to pass and score in the opposing team's end zone.

The game started with the ref wheeling onto the middle of the floor. Ace watched as Leo took their place, opposite the center from the other team. The ref tossed up the neon purple BESTBall, and Leo snagged it out of the air, securing it under their arm and already bolting toward the far end.

The audience cheered their love, and Ace joined in.

Leo was lightning on the court, which would have been cool enough all by itself—but then the court came alive. Jets of green light suddenly reached from floor to ceiling, freezing the players who hadn't been quick enough to dodge out of the beams. Leo had twisted their chair out of the way just in time, and now with most of the other team frozen, they headed toward the end zone and scored by slamming the ball against the wall square.

Ace and Emma screamed together, jumping up and down like old pals. The game continued, so wild with the speed and crash of wheelchairs—and then the added jolt of the random, brief immobilizing rays of brilliant light! Ace could watch this for years. The entire time Emma was really nice to him, and they even split a bag of neon purple sugar dough bites shaped like little BESTBalls.

It felt like he had a friend at ToP for the first time.

"Oh, get two of those! Get them!" Emma yelled when a vendor came by handing out small pieces of bright green candy. Ace grabbed two and handed one to Emma.

"You eat them right at the end," she explained.

"What do they do?"

"You'll see! It's for *sudden death*." Emma was squirming in her seat with joy. "When there's a tie . . . like there is right now!"

As the huge clock sounded the end of the quarter, Emma popped the candy in her mouth, miming for Ace to do the same. He chewed the candy and felt a little . . . weird. Emma *looked* a little weird all of a sudden. As if she were seasick or something, although she was grinning happily.

The lights went out without warning, and electric music blared through the stadium. Ace looked around at hundreds of glowing green faces. The skin of all the cadets, including his own, looked like it'd been dipped in fluorescent Bixonics tubes.

On the court, Leo was facing off with the captain of the semester three team. The neon purple BESTBall was glowing in the middle, and so were the wheels on Leo's chair and the stripes on both of their jerseys. Everything else was pitch-black!

When the tone sounded once more, Leo and their opponent shot into action, battling for the ball. Leo got it, and then got away, streaking toward the now glowing end zone. The triumphant siren of their goal made the whole stadium go stupid with screaming joy.

Ace had nearly lost his voice by the time the lights came back on and the game was truly over. Wow, why hadn't Finn told him how cool this sport was? Leo's team screamed their victory and rolled around the court to huge applause.

"Ace, you should talk to Leo about Finn." Emma leaned in close, her tone suddenly all business, just like in her vids.

Ace's last cheer died in his mouth. Emma was on a mission, and he was pretty sure it wasn't an innocent one. "Why would Leo want to know about Finn?"

"About his aug, of course. Can you imagine Leo with TurboLegs? They'd be unbeatable. A serious athlete."

Ace felt like he was speaking in slow motion. "Leo already is a serious athlete."

"Of course they are! But you know what I mean. They wouldn't have so many limitations. They could play *more* than BESTBall. They could become an all-round Auglympian."

"But—"

Emma held a hand up in front of Ace's face to stop him, and he had the oddest desire to lick it and gross her out as much as she was starting to gross him out. "I know I sound like I'm being insensitive, but Leo is only in that chair because of complications with our mom's pregnancy. They weren't supposed to be that way, you know? And TurboLegs could give Leo the kind of life they can't even imagine. We could help them imagine it."

Ace scooted away from Emma. "No thanks."

Emma's sweetness cracked. "Finn said you'd help me. Do you want me to tell him that you wouldn't help me?"

"Me going against Finn's wishes is kind of what I do best."

"He said that too. And he said it'd be a real shame if everyone here started calling you by that nickname you hate so much."

And now Ace was getting threatened. Wow.

"What's up, Emma?" a familiar voice interrupted. "Trying to corrupt our newk?"

Emma stood and faced Grayson. Ace had never been so relieved to see his boxmate. She smiled, but her voice was clipped. "I was being nice to him. Nicer than either of you two have been, I hear."

Gray looked at Ace swiftly, and Ace blinked hard. He hadn't told Emma anything about his boxmates. Who *was* this person?

"I didn't talk about our box with her," Ace rushed to say.

"I believe you," Gray said without looking at Ace. He glared at Emma. "I watched your vid about when I tried out HyperHops. Great stuff. I particularly love the way you were filming me in the tank without my permission."

Emma's cheeks got scary red. "Well, *everyone* films you. You're the ToP star." She pointed behind Gray to where, sure enough, several cadets were snapping shots of him with their watches and tablets. "Plus if I'd done something wrong, your dad wouldn't signal-boost my vids, which he did, across all the Bixonics media platforms."

"I don't think you should use my dad's ethics as a standard, Emma."

"Please, Gray, I have journalistic integrity."

"Is that what you have?" Gray shot back.

Emma held up her watch pointedly and clicked record, red light flashing. "Why *are* you so afraid of picking your aug? Does this have anything to do with the rumors about your mom's alignment with the resistance?"

"Don't you dare talk about my mom on your stupid vids."

Oh, Gray looked so mad. Ace held his breath.

Emma wasn't fazed. "How come she hasn't come forward to deny those rumors, do you think? Because they're true? She hasn't been seen in public now for, what, ten months?"

Leo rolled over, glistening with sweat and wearing a victorious smile. They stopped short in front of their twin sister, immediately sensing the tension. "Putting your nose where it doesn't belong, Emma?"

"Why are you all looking at me like that? I'm a news reporter. This is my life's work! The truth is *important*." Emma actually stamped her foot. "Why is everything I do so suspicious to you two?"

"Because you're really suspicious!" Ace yelled.

Gray and Leo cracked real smiles. Ace felt like he'd done something right for once.

"Whatever . . . *Deuce*." Emma turned and left while Ace cringed all over. Was Emma about to spread Finn's nickname around ToP? Yep. He could imagine it now. Siff would just *love* it.

Grayson's hand appeared on Ace's shoulder — in a good way. "Shake her off. She's always up to her ableist agendas. Pushy and controlling and so convinced that she's right. Emma likes to 'collect' people who are or might become famous."

Ace couldn't believe he'd shared a snack with that bottom dweller. "No wonder she likes Finn. They're perfect for each other."

Leo snapped their fingers, making both Ace and Gray stop grinding their teeth. "We beat her by ignoring her. Nothing she hates more. So, are you headed back to the box?" Leo asked Ace. "Gray can get contraband pizza. Don't ask how."

Ace nodded, afraid to say what he was dying to say and ruin this moment.

Too late.

"I can't believe you have your very own evil twin!"

Leo and Grayson stared at him. And stared. And then they laughed so hard that Ace was nearly blasted backwards by it. Gray actually tipped over on the stadium seating while he held his stomach.

Leo had little spots of tears at the corner of their eyes. They brushed them away. "That's the funniest thing anyone's ever said about her. Oh, she would *hate* it!"

They laughed for *hours*. Every ten minutes or so, one of them would repeat Ace's line and roll over laughing, and even Jayla thought it was hilarious.

That night, Ace ate the best veggie pizza he'd ever had, sitting cautiously in the center of the joy he'd created . . . by accidentally being himself. Perhaps, next time, he should do it on purpose.

11

Hercules

Aug Track: Bod
Be strong enough for *anything*.

The day had finally come. After two months of working through the level two challenges, Vaughn surprised the cadet pack by announcing that they were ready for semester one's storied test.

Time for the escape room.

"This is the big one, cadets. Consider the weeks leading up to this a warm-up. After today, you'll be assigned your trial track for the remainder of the semester, divided into three smaller groups. And you'll be working primarily with the aug assistants, who are experts at their tracks." Coach Vaughn took a deep breath when he saw Ace's hand in the air. "Wells?"

"What if the trial track isn't the right one for you?"

"You doubt my sorting methods?" Vaughn wore a quirked smile.

"I'm just thinking . . . what if? Has that happened before?"

"Then you'll get put on a different track when you start semester two."

So there was hope. If Ace came out of this assigned to Boost, maybe he could mess it up and prove that he should be Bod after all.

"Or you'll get held back and repeat semester one," Vaughn added, causing Ace's head to jerk up.

"Or get sent packing," Siff muttered, making the group chuckle in Ace's direction.

Ace ignored it, raising his hand and making strong eye contact with Vaughn. "What about the cadets who get tracked for all *three* categories?" Ace knew this was possible because of Leo. His fellow cadets, on the other hand, did not seem to know about this.

"That is rare indeed," Vaughn said. "I can think of only one cadet who's been given an open track in the last five years. One out of thousands."

Whoa.

Ace really needed to get to know Leo more. They were like a wild, promising mystery living right in his box, weren't they? Too apex for Ace? Yeah, probably.

Vaughn was giving more instructions, but Ace was distracted, going over the progress of the last few weeks. He wasn't being ignored by his boxmates anymore, but he wasn't quite in with them yet. It felt very much like he was on a trial period, after his hearty rejection of Leo's evil twin, Emma. What could he do to make it all the way into their friend group?

"Wells!" Vaughn barked. "You're already behind!"

Ace looked up and found that his entire group had lined up to file into the all-black box of the escape room. He jumped in at the end. The cadet pack filtered into a silent space that had no defining features apart from deep, impenetrable darkness.

"What do we do?" one of them whispered.

"We wait for instructions, obvs." Siff's voice was a little too close to Ace, and he backed away, finding that the door they'd come through did not have a knob on this side and even the edges of it were disappearing, as if the wall wanted to leave no trace behind.

"What could this possibly test us for?" someone asked nervously.

Ace's heart pounded. He wasn't exactly afraid of the dark, but he wasn't *not* afraid of it either. "Vaughn said there are two stages. The first must be to find some light . . . or maybe get out of this room."

"We're not supposed to work together," Siff said.

"No one said that," Ace argued back, feeling bolder in the dark.

All of a sudden everyone was talking, pushing at each other, panicking. Ace had to do something. He waved his hand in front of his face, unable to even see his fingers. Someone like Maggie might know what to do. She'd grown up with limited vision even with her glasses. "Maggie, what do you think we should do?" he asked loudly, over the alarmed voices.

"You can't just ask a visually impaired person to help you out of the dark!" Siff said.

"That's not what I was doing!" Ace yelled back. "She's good at not being able to see!"

Maggie cleared her throat. She was close to Ace. "Shut it, Siff. Ace is right. I *am* good at not depending on my eyes." Ace felt her hand catch his arm with confidence. "Everyone, find the edges of the room. Spread out, but hold hands. We need to know the perimeter. Trace it with our bodies."

After a few minutes of shuffling, the entire group was shoulder to shoulder around the room. Maggie had everyone say their names, one after the other, down the line and back to Maggie and Ace.

Ace could now tell that they weren't spread out that far at all. This space was way smaller than it seemed in Ace's mind.

"Everyone feel the wall behind you and let us know if you find anything that could be a door," Maggie said.

The reports back weren't good. No sign of a exit.

They checked the floor next, and Siff was the one to point out the last option. "It's got to be in the ceiling."

"Reach up," someone said, and Ace did—and he yelled. Everyone yelled. The ceiling wasn't out of reach like they imagined. It was barely above their fingertips. Had it closed down on them while they were in the dark?

"We have to get out of here!" Siff yelled. "Here! I've found a handle."

Everyone rushed toward Siff's voice, colliding in the center of the claustrophobic space. Ace was sweating, but he wasn't hot.

Siff cracked the door open by shoving it up, and several cadets lifted him through the narrow trapdoor. He reported back that it was in fact a new room, a room with a little bit of light, which was now pouring down on all of them. They helped each other up until the number of cadets still in the dark dwindled.

Ace helped push so many feet and legs up, and then it was just Ace and Maggie.

"That was smart thinking," Maggie said. "Up until the part where they left us."

"I can get you up there. I'm way stronger than I look." He offered his folded, locked fingers for a boost.

"But then you'll be here by yourself," she said.

"I'll find another way." Ace worked very hard to keep his voice calm and confident. Maggie had basically solved this whole room for everyone, and she deserved to be with the rest of the group. "Come on. Maybe there's something up there that you could lower down, and I could climb up?"

Maggie nodded and stepped on his hands, and he lifted her as high as he could, thinking about Mama Jay's weight training, keeping his legs bent and stomach tight so that he didn't stress out his back.

When Maggie was gone, Ace stood in the small square of light beneath the trapdoor, staring up at a room that seemed a little bit like the Brain pod room he'd visited with Jayla. It was even that same Bixonics green, which he now knew was the color of the active mainframe.

Maggie's head reappeared. "There's nothing in sight, but I'll look and come back."

She disappeared, and Ace waited as patiently as he could. Which wasn't patient at all. He paced the square of light, hearing the voices of his classmates grow farther and farther away. He tried to pull himself up, but it was too hard. Finally a head returned, but it wasn't Maggie, and Ace got a real bad feeling.

Siff smirked down at him. "That was good thinking asking Maggie."

Ace blinked. Was that a compliment?

"I should have thought of it," Siff said — and shut the trapdoor.

◳

Ace tried to grab the handle, but he was shorter than Siff, and he couldn't reach it. Not to mention that as soon as it closed, the room became pitch-black again.

And this time he was alone.

"Oh no, oh no, oh no," Ace muttered. Surely Vaughn was watching. Surely he'd come get him before Ace started screaming blindly from the terror of his own overactive imagination. Or maybe Maggie would come back. He sat on the floor in what he hoped was still the spot beneath the trapdoor. He cradled his knees and rocked. He listened to his classmates above him, shuffling around, and then they were all . . . gone! All the voices gone!

And now Ace was in the dark *and* the silence.

"Otis," he found himself whispering, pleading. "Otis!"

Otis was in the elevator, but was that all? When Ace had asked him if he knew something, he always said he knew *everything* about ToP. *Everything*, like he was already watching. "Otis, are you there? I need help. It's Ace."

"Of course it's you," Otis replied. "Your vocal patterns are an exact match. Although I am not supposed to be in this room, Ace."

"Can you help me get out? Just a little help? I won't tell anyone you helped me."

Otis was quiet for a few seconds. "The exit is now within your reach. Good luck."

Ace stood up and hit his head on the ceiling. Otis had

lowered it another foot, and not only could Ace reach the handle, but he opened the trapdoor and pulled himself up.

Not a bit about it was graceful, but he'd made it to the second stage of the escape room, and that had to mean something. He glanced around at the solid green walls and domed ceiling. Maggie was right; there really wasn't anything here.

"You did it," Maggie cried out from behind, surprising him with a hug. She was the last cadet left in the domed space. "I was waiting for you. Once the trapdoor closed, it doesn't open again from this side."

"Where did everyone go?"

"You answer five questions about the History and Theory of Human Augmentation textbook, and then you walk through the wall. That's how you know you've passed the class! I've only got one left."

Maggie looked at the wall. "Last question."

A computer voice—not Otis—spoke slowly. "The Bixonium serum is often referred to as the most revolutionary UIP in the history of humans. What does UIP stand for?"

Ace blinked blankly while Maggie thought for a moment. "User . . . interface paradigm!"

The wall changed colors in the shape of Maggie, and she stepped through as if it had become a kind of permeable solid, the Bixonics green absorbing her.

She had passed.

If Ace's heartbeat had been drumming before, it was now in double time. He had been sure that Vaughn wouldn't spring this exam on the group. They'd be given a warning, a chance to cram with that ridiculously huge textbook file straight from the devil.

"First question, please," Ace said in a rocky voice.

The computer was ready, asking about cochlear implants, which Ace knew about, but the way the computer said the questions . . . Was it trying to stump him?

His answer wasn't correct. And neither was his next one. And by the seventh question he couldn't answer—couldn't concentrate enough to answer—he'd slumped to the floor with his head squeezed between his knees. He whispered for Otis again, but this time the AI didn't return.

Ace had no idea how long he'd been there, but all of a sudden the dome of green light was gone, and he was back on the floor, sitting on a familiar gym mat as if the entire ER had dissolved around him.

Vaughn's voice floated down. "Did you give up, Wells?"

"I flunked."

"You did not pass, that is correct."

"I'm not good at questions like that. My brain shuts down. Or goes sideways. The answers all clog up and melt."

Vaughn surprised Ace by sitting on the mat next to him, which seemed like a serious challenge for the middle-aged coach. "Ace, we'll get to the second room in a minute. First I need to know how you got out of the dark room. The software went offline, and then you popped up. Did you have help from someone with XConnect?"

"Jayla didn't help me."

"Someone else maybe?"

Ace had promised not to rat on Otis. He shook his head.

Which meant he was lying to his coach.

"Did you cheat?"

"I've never cheated in my whole life." But as soon as he said the words, he immediately wondered if he was wrong. And then he remembered Vaughn's words of warning back at the pool . . . about how you could only really get kicked out of B.E.S.T. for hurting someone . . . or cheating.

Oh drudge, was asking for Otis's help *cheating?*

12

SonicBlast

Aug Track: Bod
Hear anything and everything.

The quiet weekend was a weird punishment. No news from Vaughn about Ace's fate. No news at all. Just . . . silence.

It was bad.

Really bad.

Ace couldn't stop imagining getting kicked out of B.E.S.T. He hid in his room on Saturday, tiptoeing to the bathroom when needed. For once, his boxmates were all there. Jayla kept bopping into the fridge for snacks, and Leo and Grayson played video games on the sofa. They didn't say anything, or seem to even notice him, and that's the way he wanted it.

Ace shut himself in his room again. Trying not to imagine the vidcall home. How disappointed his parents would be. How mean Finn would be about it; he'd launch into a whole round of "I told you so," no doubt.

Ace started snuffling hard, keeping it *real* quiet. He wasn't going to cry, not until he was home, with the door to his room barricaded and his head stuffed inside his pillow-case.

And so he packed.

He stuffed clothes in his duffel, as well as the odds and ends he'd hoarded in his room over his few months at ToP. An embarrassing amount of old food wrappers needed to go into the trash that he never seemed to remember to take out. When he went to the bin, he looked down at his SAR deck, still where he'd chucked it at the bottom. Pulling out the deck, he sat on the edge of the bed—and heard the knock.

"I'm busy!" His voice cracked suspiciously.

"But we've got a question only Ace would know the answer to!" Gray called.

"Okay, fine." Ace sniffed so hard his face nearly went inside out.

The door opened, and Grayson popped his head in. "What do you know about SonicBlast?"

Ace's hands did what Ace's hands always did; they shuffled the deck until the Bod aug SonicBlast, with its radioactive ear symbol, was on top. "It's like super hearing. You can hear things far away, and tune into things like a radio frequency. Perfect for musicians. You can also stop hearing things, if you want."

"I didn't actually know that last part. Good info." Grayson twisted a finger in his ear.

Ace cringed. "And . . . you're trying that one this week, aren't you?"

"Yep."

"And you heard all my snuffling."

"Like a pig in a trough."

"Grayson! Insensitive," Jayla's voice shot in from behind the door.

Gray opened the door the rest of the way, revealing Jayla and Leo peering at him. Oh no, now he'd have to explain what happened. "Can we come in?" Gray asked, eyes falling on Ace's half-packed duffel on the floor.

"Guess so."

Gray sat next to Ace while Leo rolled right up to the edge of his knees. This was starting to feel like when his parents circled him like big birds who need to snuggle and protect the messed-up little baby bird.

Jayla perched on the headboard, her crossed legs dangling off the edge. "Spill."

"I'm fine," Ace said, and the words were *everything* but fine.

"You were in the escape room yesterday," Leo said, as if diagnosing him. "And it was the worst. Most of my pack got so claustrophobic. People turned on one another. Terrible."

"I just know they're kicking me out," Ace said. "I

cheated on accident, and then I also couldn't answer any of the history and theory questions."

"Wait." Jayla held up a soft hand. "How does our in-box aug expert fail all the research questions?"

"I don't like being grilled. It's really hard. I can't always explain why so well." Ace closed his eyes tightly. "At school, before I came here, I'd listen to the teacher say all the important things, and it was like everyone else had a database in their brain to put those things away for later. Orderly folders with easy-to-access links. But it's not like that in my mind. It's like everything goes into the sinkhole, and the sinkhole is me, and there's millions of things in there, but you can't just reach in and take out the right thing all the time. The AI examiner asked me about cochlear implants, which I *do* know about, but all I could think about was magnets. Cuz, you know, they used to use magnets to hold them in place, which always seemed really cool to me, but what if you walked too close to a refrigerator? What would that feel like?"

When Ace looked up, his boxmates all wore matching high eyebrows.

"Told you, my brain doesn't take direction."

"My brain is *not* a filing cabinet. It's more like a super-computer," Jayla said. "Now a bit literally."

"Mine's an association machine," Gray said thoughtfully. "Everything connects like a huge flow chart. Maybe a map."

Leo was squinting at the wall. "My brain doesn't have any shape to it. It's a nebula." They shrugged. "I'm not at all visual."

Ace couldn't quite believe how relaxed his boxmates seemed, all thinking deeply. Also, did this mean that *everyone's* brain worked differently? If so, why was he the only one who ever seemed to have trouble? Why was he always the one who couldn't do what everyone else was doing?

Jayla started playing with her interface. The light show on her light brown skin felt like a small holiday display, with its greens and reds and blues. "Tell me about the cochlear implants, Ace. All about them. Dump out the sinkhole."

Ace did. He dived in and brought everything out. Then he started talking about how Dr. Bix invented Bixonium in his labs in California, back when he was in his early twenties, and how he didn't even know about the augmentation potential until he used it to graft a new leg onto a penguin at the zoo that had been in an unfortunate "the polar bear escaped" accident. The penguin could swim afterward and everything. His name had been Howard.

When Ace was done talking, he realized what Jayla had been doing; she was distracting him from his snuffly held-back tears. Letting him talk it all out, helping him.

Grayson had slid to the floor, sitting in front of Leo's chair while they both played with his SAR deck. Neither of them knew how to play, Ace could tell.

He moved in.

"You're not trying to get the strongest aug. You're trying to get the strongest team. It's all about how the augs work together." Ace riffled through the pile of discarded aug cards. He held up two Boosts that almost no one knew how to use in SAR. DaVinci, which significantly increased your ability to create and engineer, and Mega-Metabolism, eat nothing or everything. (Never fall victim to low blood sugar again!) "On their own these two augs are worth two points each, but if they're combined with Hercules their potential triples, as do their points."

"So they're superhero teams? This is so comic book. Dad should do ads like that. B.E.S.T.'s Avengers—or maybe that's too copycat."

Leo tossed a card down. "Honestly, Avengers was the total copycat. They appeared years after the Justice League formed, and the Justice Society was published twenty years before that."

"Maybe I wasn't suggesting the *first* superhero team, but the best superhero team," Grayson said with bite.

"You all know about comic books?" Ace yelled. "Superheroes?"

Grayson flinched big-time. "Ace! SonicBlast, remember? I can literally hear myself blink, so when you yell the paint inside my brain peels."

"Is that why you think Marvel is better than DC?" Leo played a card—a really good move, in Ace's opinion. "Because there's peeling paint in your brain?"

Grayson took the bait, eyebrows high, voice impassioned. "You know that Black Panther could erase the Justice League in an afternoon. All that Wakanda tech, add a dash of kryptonite, and bye-bye, Superman."

"Would Black Panther do that? Or would Shuri, his always-overlooked sister, do it while BP took all the credit?" Jayla asked.

Leo and Jayla fist-bumped.

Gray closed his eyes as if he was, in fact, listening to himself blink or his own pulse thunder through his veins. "My heart sounds like one of Jayla's bass rhythms. I can't wait to be done with these stupid trial augs. This is the last one."

He didn't have to add that there was only one month left in the semester, one month until graduation. One month until his birthday, until his aug surgery *had to* happen. The countdown was in the air in Lilliput. They all breathed it constantly, growing as nervous as Grayson. Ace could now understand why Jayla had been so excited and yet so messed up with fear before her surgery.

Getting an aug was huge.

Ace was pacing, still jazzed up by the idea that he'd been hiding his love of all things superhero for three months now, and all of his boxmates were cool with it. "Stupid Finn. He said everyone would call me a baby for liking comics."

"Of course we're here for it," Jayla said. "But I jam with the films and graphic novels more. Not with the DC v. Marvel eternal arm wrestle L and G are all about." She looked at Ace, motioning for him to sit down. "You all right, guy?"

"I wish I knew all this before!" Ace rifled through his half-packed duffel and took out a bunch of superhero memorabilia that he couldn't leave behind, even if he told his brother that he did. Jayla and Grayson dived at the goods while Leo cocked their head at him.

"Wait a second, did you say that Vaughn thought you were cheating?"

Ace slumped on the floor, head in hands. "Yes. No. He asked if I cheated, and I honestly don't know if I did."

"You can't cheat in the escape room," Gray said. "There's nothing in there to cheat with."

Ace had told Otis that he wouldn't tell, but Ace needed to tell someone. First he explained what had happened when they all entered the dark room. How he'd asked for Maggie's help and they'd all found the trapdoor and gotten each other out — everyone except Ace.

"Point out this Siff character for me next time we're in the cafeteria," Jayla purred in a protective voice. "The service bots might have trouble with his order."

"Okay, but go easy." Leo bit their lip. "I know Siff. I'll talk to him."

"But that's just it! It won't do any good because I won't be here. Vaughn's going to figure out that I *did* cheat and send me home. I just know it. I don't have good luck." Stiff feelings pushed right into Ace's face. He scrunched up his nose as if that might help, but it only made it worse.

"How did you get out?" Leo asked, their voice comforting.

"I asked Otis for help. The AI lowered the ceiling so that I could climb out."

Jayla stood up, all the graphic novels falling off her lap to the floor. "How in the universe did you access Otis from inside the escape room?" Her huge eyes connected with Gray's, and Ace started to panic.

"Otis is . . . my friend. I know that sounds really weird, but the AI has talked to me a lot over the weeks, especially when I couldn't find anyone else to talk with, and Otis always says the same thing: that the AI knows *everything* at ToP, so I just figured the role of elevator AI was a front. Otis is probably the mainframe protocol personality for the whole building. Kind of annoying, but really well informed."

"That's . . . genius, Ace," Leo said. "You figured that out all on your own?"

Ace only had a moment to appreciate Leo's compliment, because Gray and Jayla were having like a whole conversation without saying a word. Then they started to argue in hushed voices in the corner of his room. Ace swore he heard something about the resistance, and he couldn't help picturing that tree again, with all its strong branches and roots . . . and those protesters who had held the symbol up so very high.

When they came back, Leo locked eyes with Jayla and nodded. They turned back to Ace. "Do you think Otis would talk to you right now?"

Ace shrugged. "Um, are you there, Otis?"

"Yes, Ace, my BFF?" Otis's voice said automatically. The artificial calm in the AI's tone made his boxmates exchange wild glances. "Are you feeling all right? Your heart rate is higher than normal."

"I'm cool. Just hanging with my boxmates."

Jayla was doing something with her forearm. Speed coding. Or at least that's what it looked like.

"Hey, Otis," Grayson said. "Can you always see into our box?"

"Only when you request interface." There was a slight pause. "That tickles, Jayla."

Jayla froze. Then she went at her arm even faster.

"Thanks, Otis. We're all set here," Ace tried, wanting to get back to the joking and the superheroes. "You can go do your other jobs."

"I never stopped. I am an exquisite multitasker. Good-bye."

There was a moment when they all watched Jayla's fast fingers. When she stopped, she looked up. "Otis isn't monitoring us anymore. I broke into the Bixonics mainframe. It was like this whole box was lit up. Otis keeps an eye on you, Ace."

"You say that like . . . it's a bad thing," he managed.

Oh no, had he shared too much?

Leo touched Ace's arm. "Hey, the good news is that I'm sure that's not cheating."

"It isn't?"

"It's actually wicked smart. And shows ingenuity. Vaughn needs to know all about that to factor into his decision. You might get Brain-tracked for doing that."

"Sure, it's not your fault you figured out something you definitely shouldn't know," Jayla said under her breath.

"But I still failed that second room with all the impossible questions . . ."

"You only fail if you quit trying," Jayla said, pointing a finger at Ace. "I've got to factor all this new information into my systems." She stopped by the door. "It means that no one could get into ToP without Otis tracking them, Gray. Not even if they had the codes. *No one.*"

Gray looked really hurt by this, and Ace's brain scurried to connect the dots. Gray was hoping someone might sneak into ToP? Was Jayla helping him figure that part out? And who would he sneak in?

His mom, of course. Did that mean Gray had gotten in contact with her finally?

Jayla left Ace's room, and Leo rolled out next, saying that they wanted to help update "the plan."

Whoa, what *were* his boxmates up to?

Gray didn't leave. He looked like he needed to say something but couldn't find the words. He snapped his fingers and bounced his fists together. Finally he held up Ace's SAR deck. "Show me more about this game."

13

Scentrix

Aug Track: Boost
Super nose. Great taste. All the friends.

Ace waited to get a direct message from Vaughn or to be summoned to the head office again, but the weekend wrapped up and nothing happened—apart from teaching his boxmates how to play SAR.

When he woke up that Monday morning, the sky was smeared with purple and pink striped clouds. He turned on his tablet and checked his DMs. He *did* have a message from Vaughn, but it had been sent to everyone in his cadet pack and simply read *Today we will meet in the Coliseum.*

Seriously? But first semesters weren't allowed in the Coliseum!

Ace's heart trilled like a three-year-old banging a drum as he traveled to the level for the massive aug trial dome. It felt, a little, like returning to the scene of a crime, since this was the place where he'd nearly proven to everyone that he shouldn't be here. *This time will be different,* he promised himself. *It has to be.*

Assuming Vaughn hadn't decided to hold Ace back — or kick him out.

The cadet pack stood before the huge glass doors, and Vaughn circled everyone up.

Carlos, Alexandra, and Amir were all grinning today, like *this* was what they'd signed up for when they agreed to return as aug assistants. They had piles of wristbands in their hands, colors matching their aug track tattoos. A few blue ones for Brain in Amir's hand, slightly more Bod red ones in Alexandra's, and then Carlos had two entire fistfuls of Boost green.

"Now ordinarily, first semesters only get to see the Coliseum and have to wait until second to step inside, but *someone*" — Vaughn looked straight at Ace — "might have told Dr. Bix that it wasn't a great move to make you wait. And he agreed."

Ace blinked; he had said that to Dr. Bix's holographic frown, hadn't he? When he was ranting in his office? Whoa! He hadn't expected it to work!

"Line up with the aug track you were assigned, get your wristband, and head inside with your teaching assistant. *Listen* to them. Help each other. Be open-minded about what kind of aug you should try first. Start slow."

Bad feelings prickled all over Ace while the cadets

rushed at the aug assists. He watched Siff unhappily snap on a Bod wristband, which, first of all, was *so* surprising. Certainly Siff would be a Brain? He seemed so . . . brainy.

When the cadets had gotten their bracelets and gone into the aug dome together, Ace finally made his way to where Vaughn stood, looking down at him. "I didn't get assigned, did I? You must have sent them out this weekend. I didn't get a notice."

He tried to keep that kicked-dog whine out of his voice, but he didn't really succeed.

Vaughn exhaled for what seemed like a whole minute. "I got some messages from your friends this weekend. First, a video from screenname"—he looked at his tablet —"jayjayjoyjoy2036."

"That's Jayla, my boxmate."

"You want to see what she sent?" He flipped his tablet over and showed off a video of Ace, pacing around his room and yelling facts about cochlear implants and Dr. Bix's penguin . . . and oh drudge, it just kept *going*. "She thought this might prove that while the ER failed to get you to show off what you know, you did not fail to know it."

"I have been accused of being obsessed with this stuff, by more than one person." Ace rubbed behind his neck. *What about the first room?* He didn't manage to say it, but he did look straight at Vaughn and thought it.

"I also got a message from Grayson Bix, who needs no introduction, with a little background about your relationship with Otis. Do you know how hard it is to get the Bixonics mainframe AI to bend its programming? There have been a few XConnect cadets who have messed with Otis in the past, but AI is not programmed to trust what the young folk say or do in this skyscraper."

"Am I in trouble?"

"Not in my mind," his coach said. "You asked Otis for help. Otis gave it. You're never in trouble for asking for help at ToP. You got some good friends here. AI and real-life."

"I do?" Ace was mildly shocked. And felt embarrassingly warm all of a sudden. "So, I passed the second room, and I didn't technically cheat to get out of the first room . . ."

But I still haven't gotten assigned to an aug track.

Vaughn chuckled, clearly interpreting Ace's unsaid worry. "You're the hardest kind of cadet to sort, Wells. You ever know what's best for someone, but they aren't ready to know it, so you've got to push them along until they figure it out?"

"Ah, no. Not really." Ace cocked his head. "Wait, is that why you made Siff a Bod?"

"Siff is a trial Bod because he's too devious to head straight to Brain. He has to work his way up. Prove that he's more than selfish and self-motivated."

"So you *do* use the trial tracks to shape cadets up! That's what Leo said, my other boxmate."

"You forget I know Leo very well." Vaughn sort of smiled at Ace, and again he was hit with that warm feeling. What was this bizarre sensation? Belonging? "You're lucky to have Grayson, Leo, and"—he checked his tablet—"*jayjayjoyjoy2036* on your team."

Ace took a deep breath, closed his eyes, and held out his wrist. "Okay, assign me to Boost or Brain. I'll prove to you before second semester that I'm meant for Bod."

Vaughn snapped a wristband on Ace.

Ace opened his eyes.

It was red.

Bod red.

"Oh, Coach Vaughn!" His voice went so high so fast that he had to clear it all out and try again. "Thank you, sir."

Vaughn hooked a thumb toward the aug trial dome, and Ace threw open the huge glass doors. He ran through the Boosts, pausing to watch how Carlos's group were all trying out Scentrix, smelling things so acutely that some of them looked like they might be sick. Maggie looked particularly offended by the sharp new smell of her peers, which made Ace giggle.

But he wouldn't be distracted from the endgame. He ran as fast as he could to catch up with Alexandra and the others, where they were talking beneath the bicep logo for Bod. The carpet beneath his feet was a lush red to match the wristband. Ace hadn't noticed that last time he was here. He checked the high tower for SuperSoar, where he'd made the terrible decision not to listen to his friends.

That wouldn't be happening again.

◻

"You can try out one aug today," Alexandra was saying to the small group. "Choose wisely. Don't go straight to the TurboLegs, because *everyone* goes straight there, and really, what's the fun of running wicked fast?" Ace laughed, and Alexandra winked at him. They must have had a few run-ins with Finn, pun intended. "Okay, pair up."

Famous.

Last.

Words.

Ace closed his eyes and said a tiny little hope chant. By the time he'd opened them, he realized it was far too late. No one really wanted to be partners with Siff—just like no one really wanted to be partners with Ace. They were a match made by a supervillain.

Siff actually growled as he walked over to Ace, after the rest of their group had shot off in different directions. "All right, drudge. Let's head to SuperSoar."

Ace's mouth tipped open slightly. "You want to try out my favorite aug with me?"

"Of course I don't want to! But I clearly got on Vaughn's bad side. I should *not* be a Bod. My whole box agrees. I'm Brain material, and I'm being punished. My dad told me that smart people are always punished because they can handle more than everyone else."

Ace decided it was best to say nothing to that. Siff and Ace headed toward the SuperSoar tower, finding a Bixonics technician waiting to help them out. First they watched a holographic instruction set of someone climbing the tower and using SuperSoar, which made it look so easy.

Next, the tech fitted the two cadets with the harnesses that Ace really shouldn't have thought were optional last time around. After that, they strapped this light metal framework with parachute film on Ace's back, connecting down along his arms. Ace's heart beat so fast that it was hard to hear the instructions.

He was only supposed to glide, no flapping yet. Okay, he got it.

But what he really got was a beautiful daydream. It had been weeks since Ace had let himself imagine flying. Spreading his wings over the rooftops of his hometown, soaring, the breeze beneath his arms. In these visions, he was faster than Finn, because as the crow flies was always shorter! And Ace was always spying on the ground in these daydreams, looking for anyone who needed help. A *real* superhero.

The tech finished outfitting Siff and then sent them

to the foot of the tower. They were supposed to spot each other, like they'd been doing for weeks on the climbing wall. But Ace hadn't been paired with Siff before, and to be honest, Ace's archnemesis wasn't going to be that invested in keeping Ace from crashing into the ground.

"Well," Siff spat. "What are you waiting for? Isn't this the biggest moment of your life? You haven't quit talking about it since you got here."

Ace nodded and went to the foot of the tower.

"First platform *only*," the technician called out.

Ace knew why. The first platform was only about fifty feet up. He'd gone halfway to the third platform on the tower when he'd gotten frozen by fear last time. He climbed easily, Siff letting out slack on the line tethering them together through a high loop.

Once on the first platform, Ace lifted his arms. The hardware was so light and yet already felt so powerful. When he got SuperSoar, all the metal would be planted in his bones and the parachute fabric would become a kind of skin he could call up — like one of those flying squirrels who didn't seem to have wings, but then shot out of the tree at a great height, gliding down to earth.

Ace stood at the edge of the platform. He had a pretty good view of the entire trial dome from here. Everyone was having a blast, and he took a moment to pat his own back. He'd made this happen — on accident, of course — when he'd ranted at Dr. Bix that fateful night back at the start of the semester. Maybe there was a good reason that it had been so hard to get here, to this spot, wearing this gear, on the edge of everything exciting. And sure, Siff was his partner, but maybe even that could sort itself out. Maybe he could help Siff prove to Vaughn that he was supposed to be Brain.

They could even be friends.

"Jump already, drudge!" Siff shouted up at him.

Then again, maybe not.

Ace thought about everything the technician had told him, but it was already starting to smash into his sinkhole with everything else. They'd said the first platform *only*, to glide, that Siff's weight would keep him safe if the wings didn't catch the air right—just like they'd practiced on the climbing wall all semester. There was something else to remember, but those were definitely the big ones.

Ace held out his arms, took a deep breath, and jumped.

The wings filled in half a second—and Ace didn't fall.

He glided, tilting a tiny bit and turning in a whole circle. It wasn't fast like Ace had imagined. The feeling was much softer and more peaceful. This felt like the slowest Ace had ever moved in his life, and also the very *best*.

Halfway down to the ground, Ace wasn't ready to be done.

So he flapped his arms.

Just once.

And shot up like a rocket, hitting the end of his tether

to Siff and jerking backwards. Everything felt wrong, there was no air under his wings, and he was falling for real. Siff had slipped when Ace's weight had jerked the line so hard, and therefore Siff wasn't braced and flew up in the air . . .

. . . and Ace *crashed hard.*

14

MetaMorph
Aug Track: Boost
Heal fast. Adapt in a pinch.

The bad news: two broken shinbones. Two. As in *both of them*.

Ace now understood why the MetaMorph aug was so popular. Healing took forever . . . even with the universe-altering Bixonium serum. In aug surgeries, the serum was used to graft technology and titanium hardware to bones, but in Ace's case, the Bixonium simply grafted his splintered bones back together. The process included a whole lot of injections (*owww*), three days bed rest on the hospital level of ToP, and sooo many calls from his parents.

Ace had learned a lot about the hospital level. First of all, for a student program, this place had an awfully huge medical complex. It rivaled the megahospitals he'd visited when he was little and Mom had been so sick. She was okay now, but the scent of disinfected air and shine of scrubbed surfaces and all that quiet pain had left a shivering impression on Ace.

Also surprising was that not everyone here was a student recovering from aug surgeries or plain old colds and flus — or stupidity, in Ace's case. There was a whole wing filled with older people, as old as thirty-seven, he guessed, because they all had aug tattoos that tracked with the first class of augmented humans, some twenty-four years ago.

What were they all doing here? Were there problems with augs when people got older?

Nah, if something like that were true, everyone would know.

Ace's tablet flashed with a call from home. "Hi," he said, holding it up so his moms could see his pointedly smiling face. "I'm doing everything the doctor says, and apparently I'm healing faster than the average dual broken tibias."

Mama Jay was holding the tablet close and her face was extra round from the camera angle. "We're coming for the night!" He could tell he was still in trouble because he'd engaged full Mama Bear Mode. Mom was always worried about something, but when Mama Jay was growling, he knew to tread lightly. "I'm packing right now."

"You are not, Jay. Talk to him like a grownup!" Mom called from the other room. She had actually been the chill one since *the accident*. Another sign that this was no small mistake in Ace's mistake-ridden young life.

"How do you feel? Are your friends visiting? Do you need anything?" Mama Jay fired.

"I've had loads of visitors." Ace's boxmates had come by yesterday, that part was true, but he did wonder what his now-tracked cadet pack was up to. No doubt he was missing all the cool orientations to Bod. Hopefully Alexandra would catch him up once he was healed. "Honestly, I just need the peace and quiet."

"He's lying," Finn said from somewhere offscreen. "I'll run down and check on him."

"Not so fast, Finn. You need to clean your room before you're allowed out," Mom said in that no-nonsense voice, which actually warmed Ace's heart just a little. At least Ace wasn't the only one on probation with their parents. Mom's smiling face appeared in the camera, lovingly pushing Mama Jay's grump to the side. "Are you sure you don't need anything?"

"I'm okay," Ace said with a shrug that seemed to tattle on him. Or was it his tone of voice giving him away? His parents exchanged concerned looks.

"Hey, Ace," Grayson said from behind the curtain. "You awake?

"See? I have to go. My boxmate Gray is here."

"Grayson Bix?" Finn barked, stepping into the frame. "Does he actually hang out with you or is this a pity visit? Does he know about your collection of superhero capes?"

"Byeeeee!" Ace yelled, hitting the end button before Finn could get more digs in. "Come in, Gray."

Grayson parted the curtain with one eyebrow hooked high. "What's this about capes?"

"My first real collection," Ace explained. "I've got the Hollywood replicas from all the A-list caped heroes and a few B ones too. A whole wall of heroes in my bedroom at home."

"Superman?"

"Please. He was the first."

"Thor?"

"Course."

"Mx. Fire-Eater?"

"Tenth birthday score."

Gray's approving grin meant everything. "I'd love to see that sometime."

Ace couldn't believe he didn't have to hide things like this from Grayson. In fact, the more he acted like his plain old superhero-obsessed self, the more Gray relaxed around him.

Gray held up a small to-go box. "You're missing the Diwali celebration. I brought you some *chiroti*."

"Thanks. I didn't even know the festival was happening."

"The BIPOC organizations have lots of celebrations. Some of them are open to the whole program, like this one. I'll let you know next time one comes up."

Gray sat and fussed with his ear; he probably had the trial SonicBlast aug in again.

"How's the great aug debate of 2048?" Ace asked carefully. Gray never wanted to talk about his trial augs, but he was running out of time before his birthday — and the last possible day he could have his aug surgery.

Gray rubbed the back of his neck. "Well, I ruled out HyperHops and FelineFinesse last week. Just can't get used to accidentally jumping three feet in the air when I get hiccups." He shivered. "And I kept poking Leo with the cat tail when we were watching a movie. Too weird." Grayson's voice went all pebbly and then he glanced everywhere but at Ace.

Ace was at a loss to interpret such behavior, although it did remind him of when Maggie had come to visit yesterday and brought him a BESTBall candy, since he'd missed the game. Why was the ceiling so interesting when she was there? Also the floor. And all the other patients.

"Want to play?" Gray reached for Ace's worn-through SAR deck. He dealt the cards, five each to start. Ace looked at his hand. All Boosts, which was not great, but he could work with it. Gray and Ace took turns trading out their least favorite aug and picking up new ones, creating a discard pile that actually told Ace a lot about Gray's hand. He was trying to build an all-Bod pack, which was a safely strong move. Too predictable, however.

Ace picked up the Sherlock card by luck. Gray was dead now. The Sherlock aug, Brain track, was one of the best cards in the deck, as it multiplied the points of most of the other cards by four. The only better card was iNsight, the rando Boost aug that could basically magnify any other augs simply by being tuned in to human emotions. There were no limitations to this card's bonus — it multiplied them all by *five*. By itself, however, the card was worth only one point. The only card in the deck worth one point.

Ace called the battle, and Gray played his Bods.

Ace placed his four cards and said the winning words, "Some assembly required."

Gray threw his hand down. "How do you do that so fast?"

"Like, way too many years playing with my brother, before he went to B.E.S.T. and got too cool to do anything fun ever again." Ace paused and grinned at Gray. "Actually, he won't play with me anymore because he can't beat me, and he's a total toddler when he loses."

"We all know who the real baby is, Deuce."

Ace closed his eyes and cursed. Finn was standing at the foot of his level 101 bed, a light sheen of sweat on his temple, as if he'd broken some world record in getting here. Honestly, he probably had.

"You're not supposed to be here!" Ace said. "I'll tell moms."

"Tattling so fast in front of your new pal? That's drudgy, little bro." Finn zipped over to Grayson and held out his hand to shake. "Hey, Gray. We ate lunch a few times together before I graduated. You might remember."

Grayson looked at Ace for a sec before he shook Finn's hand. "Yeah, I remember you."

"I hear you're a fellow Bod." Finn looked all over for evidence of Grayson's aug choice. Joke was on Finn because Gray didn't have one yet. "Have you . . . not selected still?"

Ace scoffed. Finn was definitely watching Emma's ToP news vids, and therefore knew all about Gray's delayed decision, so this was just one of Finn's aloof celebrity acts.

Grayson rubbed his face and exhaled. "I'm leaning VisionX or SonicBlast."

"Tasteful," Finn said, which sounded anything but, coming from his mouth.

Gray glanced at Ace and rolled his eyes. Ace tried not to laugh, and Finn noticed.

Finn took a few steps forward and pushed at Ace's legs with one finger. It didn't hurt, but it wasn't kind either. "You know, I had the same braces when I was recovering from my TurboLegs surgery. Course, mine were bigger. You've got such skinny legs."

Ace and Gray exchanged another glance. "Told you, he's a big-bro bully stereotype. Can't help himself."

Finn was getting more aggravated by the second, and while Ace was kind of enjoying it, he was also worried that this could explode. Finn was dangerous when he didn't feel like a star.

"You're such a pain in the butt. I only came here to tell you I've thought up a new nickname for you, like you always wanted. We can retire Deuce. From this day forward, you shall be known as" — Finn waved his hand as if delivering a grand headline — "Code Name Icarus."

Whatever reaction he was waiting for — most likely Grayson's laughter — didn't happen.

"Are you referring to the Greek myth?" Gray asked. "That's a stretch, don't you think?"

Finn's cheeks pinked. "It's funny. Because he went to fly and totally crashed."

"Is it funny that your brother broke both of his legs?"

Now that pink was turning bright red. "No, but he's *fine*."

Ace's tablet started to ring — another call from home. He held it up. "They're looking for you. You're in trouble now. Better run back and clean your room."

Finn muttered through his teeth, and then pinched Ace's ear on his zooming, blurred way out of level 101.

Gray was shaking his head. "What an exceptionally drudgy person."

"He's got a big-sibling complex. I think it's because

I remember when he wasn't so confident and a national hero. He hates that I know the *before* side of him." Ace was surprised by a quick stab to the chest and memories of snowball fights and SAR games. And the time they both wore capes and leaped off the couch shouting their own heroic taglines.

Gray's voice woke him up. "That's pretty emotionally advanced, Ace."

"I've been in therapy since my teacher couldn't get me to sit in the circle with all the other kindergartners. Mama Jay says I have an 'advanced degree in feelings.'"

"That's got to come in handy."

"To be honest, Finn hasn't been the same since he came back from B.E.S.T. My parents blame being a teenager. I think it's more. Like he got augmented on the inside as well as the outside." Ace didn't realize what he was implying until it was too late. "I don't mean there's anything wrong with your dad's—"

"I get what you mean," Gray said, one more time looking like his thoughts were paused on something Ace didn't know about. Gray shuffled the SAR deck. "Your parents are cool, aren't they? I always wondered what it'd be like to have two moms."

"Really? I always wondered what it would be like to be Black," Ace said, wincing. He wasn't sure if that was insensitive or not. "Sorry!"

Gray laughed hard, but the sound had another feeling

mixed in as well. Ace swore it was so real, he could have picked it up with his hands. His boxmate was *really* sad about something.

"Gray . . . why don't you want to pick your aug?"

Grayson dealt the cards. "It's not actually about the augs. It's more like . . . once I pick, it's all over. Permanent. No going back. And that means graduating, leaving, going home."

"To your parents?"

"To my dad's place in Switzerland. My parents are divorced, which is really good. They do *not* get along." He scratched at his hair above his ear. "But I haven't seen my mom in a long time, so that sucks. And my dad is always working. You've met him. Well, holograph him, which is pretty much the only version I see these days."

Oh. Yeah, that would mess up Ace's feelings too.

Gray fussed with his ear again. "I don't want to graduate and leave ToP and Leo. Dad'll put me on tour or something. To show off my aug in every major city in Europe."

"Why don't you come back as an aug assist?" Ace asked. Gray looked confused, as if the idea had never occurred to him. "Bet your dad would agree, wouldn't he? That'd be great press, like you're always saying he wants."

"Yeah, maybe." Gray seemed mildly cheered on by the idea, and Ace felt good.

They played SAR, and Ace waited a while to ask his

lingering question. "So who was Icarus? Some kind of demigod?" Ace added hopefully.

"He was just a guy who had wings made from wax and feathers. Crashed because he flew too close to the sun. His wings melted."

"Icarus clearly needed a cape."

"All the Greek stories end pretty badly. Apparently getting too proud of your power is the fastest way to lose it." Grayson dealt another hand, and Ace thought about letting him win. "Ace, that stuff with Finn, that little brother chip on your shoulder? You got to get rid of it. How are you going to learn to fly with all that weighing you down?"

Ace closed his eyes, the words he'd held back since the doctor had announced his twin broken legs busting out. "But Vaughn won't even let me try SuperSoar again, will he? I think I blew it." Ace's tablet hummed with another notification before Gray could say anything. He checked the screen. "Oh no."

"What is it?"

"New Emma vid. *Eww*, this one's called 'The Love Report.'"

Grayson threw down his cards. "It's one of her gossipy special segments because of the Misey dance next week. Better watch to make sure she isn't up to anything." He tapped play. "She loves to talk about how I'm still 'unattached' for all those cadets nursing crushes."

"I do not like dances," Ace said, just as Emma's pleased,

controlled face projected above Ace's tablet. He barely watched as Emma started reporting on all the couples at ToP, shuffling his cards instead. It was pure gossip, and Ace had no idea how she got away with this stuff—but when her voice turned downright gleeful, he got a sudden bad feeling and had to watch.

Emma's grin was tricky. Daring. "And last, it's my *pleasure* to report that love might finally be in the air for ToP's own golden prince, Grayson Bix, and everyone's favorite star on the BESTBall court . . ."

Grayson leaned way forward. So did Ace.

Emma cut to a video of Grayson and Leo sitting side by side in the cafeteria, elbowing each other playfully and talking with their faces close together. Even to Ace, it looked friendly . . . but also very flirty.

Grayson stood up, turned in a full circle, and rushed away.

LEVEL THREE:

BE YOURSELF

15

MegaMetabolism

Aug Track: Boost
Eat anything or nothing. Survive in hazardous
places.

Ace was in the dark again, but this was no escape room.
Jayla's laser labyrinth in the Brain track holo-room was
maybe the coolest thing he'd ever done at ToP—a surprise present she'd programmed just for the Lilliputians.

And it was gravity-free.

He wore a jumpsuit that felt like something that should
accompany space flight, and he could not figure out how
to keep himself right-side up. In truth, he'd actually forgotten which side *was* up. He zoomed around as if he were
flying, pushing off the walls, spinning around. Without
realizing it, his arms shot out as if he had the SuperSoar
trial aug on again.

After a few minutes, he pulled up his mask, finding
only the neon green walls of the Bixonics holo-room. The
walls, floor, and ceiling were similar to the pod room he'd

visited with Jayla—where he almost accidentally called the parents she *wasn't* in touch with—only this one had a huge labyrinthine layout and a variety of gravity settings. Everything from no-grav, for space simulations, to heavy-G, for aug training that involved intense muscle development.

He put the mask back down and the room washed black with neon specks, making it feel like outer space, or maybe the bottom of the ocean. After three days in bed, this was *exactly* what he'd needed to feel better, to get his head back in the program for the last two weeks of the semester.

The only problem was that he was starving. He suddenly understood why cadets went for MegaMetabolism, shutting their hunger on and off. Ace thought about checking to see if his boxmates wanted to head to the cafeteria after this, but that only called attention to a much bigger problem . . .

His boxmates were not in great shape. Ace had returned from level 101 to find Leo and Grayson avoiding each other —which was super awkward when you all live in the same place. Apparently Emma's 'Love Report' had caused a real rift between them, or at least that's what Jayla had called it. Which was another reason that she'd spent all this time writing the software to turn the holo-room into an outer space adventure to bring everyone back together.

Ace certainly needed the pick-me-up after Otis filled

him in on everything that had happened to his cadet pack now that they had their track assignments. The Bods had tackled that amazing obstacle course without him, the Brains were deep in their avatar work, and the Boost cadets were going through a bunch of trials to discover their strongest skill to, well, boost.

At first Ace had felt left out. But now, with his box-mates all around him, things didn't seem so bad. When Leo shot in like a missile, Ace was weightlessly spinning in a circle, smiling hugely.

"Would it hurt if I said I really hope you get your wings, Ace?"

He winced. "You mean hurt because it's such a long shot?"

Leo didn't respond because they were gone before Ace finished the question. They were fast without gravity. Like on the BESTBall court, they seemed to know how to get places quickly and with the least amount of energy.

Jayla and Grayson came around the corner next. Both of them were using magnets on their boots to take huge astronaut-style steps. Ace tried not to notice the way Leo pushed themself to the far side of the room at the sight of Gray, as if suddenly needing to examine something. Grayson pulled the same move, but to the opposite corner.

Jayla unlocked her boot magnets and sent herself floating up to meet Ace. "What do we do about them?" she asked in a whisper. "I thought for sure this would get them interacting again. This was our favorite hangout spot last semester."

Ace shrugged. "I think this misery dance—"

"Misey," Jayla corrected.

"Yeah, well I think it's broken everyone's brains. I've gotten asked to go by three people. You know I'm up for everything at ToP, but . . ." He held his hands up, palms out. "Ace does not do dances."

"Three people? And you said you weren't popular!" Jayla shoved his shoulder, and it sent Ace into a backflip. They shared a laugh that echoed through the zero-G room.

"I think we've just got to get everything between Leo and Gray out on the table. No more unspoken weirdness. In my family, we put it all out there. Even if it means hurt feelings." Jayla paused, scowling, and then clapped her hands and hollered at her boxmates. "Okay, bring it in!"

Gray and Leo reluctantly joined Ace and Jayla in the middle of the room. Unfortunately, Leo was floating twenty feet in the air and Gray's feet were firmly locked to the floor.

"What is it?" Leo asked.

Jayla cracked her knuckles. "Sound off. Who's going to the dance?"

"Not me!" Ace shouted, happy to get that out there.

Gray glanced at Leo and opened his mouth, but Leo beat him to it.

"I'm going with a first semester."

Gray looked stunned. "But we always go together. You won't go with me just because Emma made that video?"

Leo did a very Leo thing. They looked away, and shrugged. "I've got other plans."

Ace didn't think the tension in the room could get any worse, but then a tree appeared in the middle of the floor. A huge, flowering tree. It looked just like the symbol from the resistance.

"It's beautiful, Jayla!" Ace said.

"Um, I'm not doing that." Jayla had started running her fast fingers along her interface. "A signal piggybacked on my network to avoid Bixonics's security. It's coming from outside ToP."

Grayson and Leo forgot their weirdness, drawing close. All four of them were staring at the tree.

"She's trying to reach out to you," Jayla whispered to Gray, and somehow Ace knew they were talking about Gray's missing mom.

"Are you sure it's her?" Gray asked. "It could be your parents."

"Either way we have to check. We have to open the channel."

Leo grabbed Ace by the elbow and flew them both through the zero-grav to a different room in the labyrinth. "Better if you don't know what they're about to do."

If being bonded with his boxmates had kept him from

feeling left out before, he was definitely feeling it now. "Can I at least know more about that symbol?"

"Tree of life. Originally an important image to Celtic people."

Ace couldn't stop himself from asking. "But it's the resistance symbol now, isn't it?"

"No wonder Vaughn has trouble with you." Leo gave him a good smile, quickly changing the subject. "You're pretty smart. Too smart to be wasted on a Bod aug. Have you thought about Brain?"

Ace checked Leo's strong arms for the three bracelets he'd noticed the first day he met them. A red for Bod, green for Boost, and blue for Brain. "Leo, can I ask you about being tracked to all three categories?"

They snapped the bracelets absentmindedly. "It's not as glamorous as it sounds. I don't really have a cadet pack because I switch groups every week or so. Friends are important in this place." Leo's voice twisted with misery.

"Emma shouldn't have made that vid," he tried, and Leo's eyes snapped to meet his.

"Don't worry about her. I'll take care of Emma."

Ace's mouth hung open as he realized that this was not the kind of hole he could dig himself out of. He scrambled for a new topic and found his biggest fear sitting right there, waiting. "Hey, so, Vaughn tracked me for Bod but he also made it sound like he thought I should be on a different track. After what happened in the Coliseum, I'm worried he's going to switch me to Brain." *Not Boost, please not Boost.* "You had Vaughn. What do you think I should do?"

"You know his secret, right? You figured it out. Tell me you figured it out."

"What secret? Does it have something to do with that tree symbol?"

"No, no. Forget about that symbol. That's not for you to mess with or know about." Leo had never talked so harshly to Ace before. He didn't know what to say. Luckily, they softened their tone and continued. "As for Vaughn . . . if you haven't figured it out, I'm not going to tell you, but you should pay attention to him."

◙

Leo and Ace waited almost an hour for Gray to finish up with whatever he wasn't supposed to know about. When Gray left scowling, Ace was pretty sure the call hadn't worked. A few moments after Gray stormed out of the labyrinth, Leo followed in the same direction. It might be a sign that the two of them were going to patch things up.

Ace hoped it was a sign.

Jayla floated over to him. "That's enough stress. Let's go somewhere pretty." She changed the settings on her interface and the black, spacey, gravity-free environment melted into a soft field of white wildflowers before a long, sandy beach.

Ace's feet touched down slowly, and he felt a breeze through the suit, which mimicked environments. It used all five senses, so he could even smell the ocean. "This is lovely! Where are we?"

"A place from one of my memories." Jayla sat hard in the flowers, trailing her fingers through them. "Sit, Ace." Ace dropped down cross-legged. She grinned and scrunched her nose. "Sometimes you seem so young, you know that?"

"Young at heart, or so I've been told."

"We're all worried about you. This place isn't easy, and it isn't always safe. You have to be on guard from . . . a lot of stuff. And while we're still in my mainframe and no one in ToP can hear us, I have to tell you something. I'm not sure you should trust Otis. In fact, I know you shouldn't."

Ace's shoulders drooped. If he couldn't trust Otis, that pretty much meant he couldn't trust B.E.S.T. Or Coach Vaughn. Or Dr. Bix. And that was way too much to distrust.

Jayla got up and walked around a corner in the holoroom, beckoning for Ace to follow. They were now inside a really nice house. Ace and Jayla walked around the old, sort of perfect rooms. The walls and floors felt as weathered and inviting as a piece of driftwood. All the furniture looked like it had been in the same spot for a hundred years already, settled in for a hundred more.

Ace found a family portrait on the wall. Even though she was a little bit younger in the picture, it was clearly Jayla with her mom and dad. Jayla and her dad had the same brown skin and wide, happy smiles. Her mother's look was much more serious.

Ace touched the wooden wall. It felt real. "This is your home?"

She turned abruptly as if prepared to deny it, but then shrugged. "It's the place where I grew up. My family doesn't live here anymore. I don't actually know where they are. They keep off the grid. Dad's the nerdiest scientist you ever met, but he also taught me tae kwon do. Mom is a real military type. Business and order and results."

Jayla seemed both annoyed and relieved to be talking about them.

"Can't you find them? With your XConnect?" Ace asked, puzzled. He was pretty sure there wasn't anything Jayla couldn't do.

"Maybe. But they don't want to be found. I'm here without their permission." Her voice was soft but her words were not. They felt as heavy and inflexible as Mama Jay's weights.

"Your family didn't want you to get augged?" Ace asked, trying not to stare up at her with big cartoon eyes, but knowing that that was how he probably looked.

She patted his helmet. "No, Ace. They didn't want me

to come here. They would have stopped me if they could, but I ran away."

Ace remembered the protesters with the angry signs in front of ToP all those months ago. He tried to picture her family among them, but he couldn't. Maybe he didn't want to. "Can you go home . . . after you get augged?"

Jayla looked at him sharply. "Of course I can. They'll want me back." Her words started out confident and then slowed and quieted . . . as if she was trying to convince herself that it would all work out, when the truth was that it might not. It might not at all.

Ace felt a pang in his chest and wanted to say something encouraging, but Jayla ended the program. The room washed the berry-blue color of her mainframe, and then she even turned that off, returning the holo-room to that vivid, Bixonics green color that was everywhere at ToP.

As if the AI had been waiting for Ace to pop back up in the system, Otis's voice loudly announced, "Ace Wells, Coach Vaughn is waiting for you in his office."

Jayla's eyes flew wide. "*Oof.* That doesn't sound good."

□

Vaughn's office was overflowing with SAR stuff. There were shelves upon shelves of collectible card sets. He even had the limited edition figure sets for all the Bixonics aug stars. Ace had dreamed about rooms like this.

Vaughn sipped black coffee from behind a desk. "Sit, Wells. Feeling better?"

"Yeah, good as new." Ace's eyes trailed to a B.E.S.T. diploma framed on the wall, right beside a picture of Vaughn with the president of the United States. "Wait. What? You know the president?"

"We were boxmates," he said, glancing back at the image. "Want the inside scoop? She's as cool as you think she is. And she's also hard as steel when she needs to be."

Ace nodded knowingly, even though he still couldn't picture Coach Vaughn hanging out with the president. It was like Ace trying to imagine going to the Misey dance with any of the people who'd asked him. Just sort of . . . impossible.

He pointed to another picture, this one of a much younger Vaughn and Jeck Misey. As in the *Misey dance.* As in the dance he'd just been thinking about. "You know him too? Wait, but you don't have an aug tattoo! How . . ."

Ace smacked a hand over his face. "How could I forget? The first class of B.E.S.T. cadets got their aug tattoos on the back of their necks." He peered at Vaughn as if he might be able to see straight through to behind his collar. "So you were in the first cadet pack! Brain or Bod? I'm betting Brain because you are so good at figuring out people's aug tracks. Oh, do you have the Sherlock aug like the president? Is that how you're so good at decoding people?"

"People aren't codes, Wells." Vaughn's demeanor was serious now. Serious as in *remember how you were called to my office.*

Ace tried to beat him to the punch. "I know I shouldn't have flapped with SuperSoar. I learned so much in just one try. I'm sure that next time I—"

"Ace." Vaughn's tone made Ace's plea shut off like a faucet. When his coach spoke again, his voice had quieted. "I heard a rumor that you're amazing at SAR."

"I'm . . . pretty good." Ace didn't want to brag, especially in front of someone whose room was covered in so many cards they were basically wallpaper.

Vaughn took out a deck and dealt with speed. Ace picked up his cards, finding the luck of the draw. He'd gotten iNsight. The Boost aug that, when combined with supporting augs, turned into an unbeatable hand. He looked at the card with its glowing, silvery foil, blank with possibility. Or at least, that's always what Ace had seen when he'd drawn it.

Ace and Vaughn silently discarded their two rounds, and Ace kept his eye on the discard pile. This wasn't like playing with Gray, who went for all muscle, or Jayla, who hoarded Brain cards, or even Leo, who was really good at strategizing because they weren't predictable. Vaughn was unreadable as he arranged his math points . . . but he definitely seemed sure of himself.

In the end, the coach had dealt Ace the best card in the deck, but before he could set down his pack, Vaughn said, "You won."

"How do you know?"

"Because you're jittering with excitement. I can feel it."

"Some assembly required." Ace set down his winning pack. Vaughn *could* feel it, couldn't he? Not because he was simply empathetic by nature like Ace, but because he had an aug for it. "*You* have iNsight. You can track other people's emotions."

"It isn't so much a process of tracking. More like creating a map. People live their lives in a way that makes patterns in their own minds, roads built on feelings. Good ones, bad ones. All of them. As a coach, this skill set is invaluable. I can push my cadets to do their best, while always being aware of their breaking point."

"So that's how you took one look at me and knew that I was desperate to be a Bod?"

"No, Ace. I took one look at you and knew that you were noticing everyone else." Vaughn leaned back, hands clasped around his mug. "I've only tracked three cadets for iNsight in the decade I've been doing this. I do believe you're my fourth."

Ace shook his head. Left and right didn't seem like

enough, so his head went up and down and every direction of *no, thank you, not even a little.*

"This is going to hurt me a lot more than it hurts you." Vaughn paused and almost laughed. "Literally, because I sense all my cadets' emotions whenever they're near me." He turned on his tablet and typed something. Ace's Bod-red wristband flickered, and then turned green.

Boost green.

Ace's sudden grief was everywhere. Inside of him, but also somehow melting down the outsides of his body.

When he looked up, Vaughn had tears in both eyes. He gave Ace a very tight smile. "You can earn your Bod track back with a little open-mindedness."

"I am never trying iNsight!" Ace shouted. "I don't want to know more about people's feelings. They're already all over me all the time! Also, you cannot be any kind of hero by knowing how other people feel."

"It's not about knowing. It's about helping. What you do with the information you're already receiving as a naturally empathetic person who has strong mirror neurons." Vaughn motioned to the cards. "Didn't you just win with iNsight? Didn't it bring out the best in all the other augs in your hand? How is that not heroic?"

"It's just a game," Ace said miserably, eyes glued to the green of his wristband.

"Then maybe it's time for this to be more than a game."

16

NerveHack

Aug Track: Brain
You don't have to feel pain. Ever again.

The next morning, Ace reported to his cadet pack at the Coliseum, trying to hide his green wristband beneath a long-sleeved shirt. Which wasn't even that necessary because the only thing anyone could talk about was the upcoming dance.

Ace filtered through the great glass doors with his eyes high. Looking swiftly away from the SuperSoar tower—his unique place of shame at this point—his eyes settled on the Bod symbol. He wouldn't be allowed over there today.

And he wasn't the only one.

"How did I get switched?" Siff was yelling at Vaughn, waving a green wristband. "I go to sleep Bod and wake up Boost? What did I do? I didn't do anything!"

Vaughn looked over his tablet, definitely not impressed by Siff's volume and attitude. Ace wondered what it was like for Vaughn, having to sense Siff's feelings whenever he was around. "Perhaps your journey isn't about you." His tone was stiff. "Find your partner and get to work."

Ace winced as Siff felt the undercurrent in those words. Siff glared at Ace's wristband, also green, and stormed over. He held out his arm. "This is about you, isn't it? What did you do?"

"Honestly, I think it's about both of us. Vaughn wants me to try Boost before I commit to Bod, and he wants you to get along with me . . . before you get your coveted Brain track."

Siff squinted as if Ace gave him a headache just by existing. "Okay, let's go try out the Boosts. Maybe if I help you, he'll change his mind about me."

Siff and Ace walked over to the Boost section of the Coliseum. Even though it was bigger than the other two sections, it was mildly overrun. Boost was by far the most common aug track. There were two Boost cadets to every Bod. Three to every Brain.

First, they passed the huge aquarium with over a dozen cadets swimming about, trying out GillGraft, which allowed the lungs to pull oxygen as a gas right out of the water. Ace had always been fascinated by the science behind that particular aug, but since he lived far from the underwater cities in the middle of the ocean, it wasn't high on his list to try.

Carlos was demonstrating how he could climb inside

a space the size of a clothes dryer with UltraFlex in front of several fascinated cadets who kept daring him to get in smaller and smaller containers. Beyond that, Siff and Ace lost at least twenty minutes watching Maggie paint a perfect replica of Van Gogh's *Starry Night* with the DaVinci trial aug, which amped up any artistic talent to incredible heights. Unofficial tagline: the unlimited muse.

"Want to try it?" Siff asked, breaking the little reverie that Ace had slipped into while Maggie swirled the stars with yellow and surprising white accents.

"Nah," Ace said. "I've got no natural artistic abilities. I went through a phase where I was drawing my own comic books, and Mama Jay kept being like, 'This is great . . . but what is it?'"

Siff snorted a laugh that didn't feel like it was aimed at Ace like a torpedo. Was this progress? "So, what does Vaughn want you to try? If he needs you to test Boost, he must have some clue as to where your aptitude lies. The faster we get that done, the faster you get back to Bod, and I get to Brain."

Ace considered lying to Siff while they wandered through the Coliseum. That's how much he did not want to head to the empty iNsight station.

Siff got impatient. "MegaMetabolism? Because you're skinny? Or SenseXL? How's your nose? Ever felt like you need your five senses to be incredibly strong?"

Ace shook his head. He pointed.

"iNsight?" Siff asked incredulously. "No one picks iNsight. Its only claim to fame is winning SAR."

"Now you know why he had to trick me into trying it!" Ace snapped. "Of course I don't want to try it out, but I guess I don't have a choice."

"We'll make it fast," Siff said, almost as if he was supporting Ace on this—but also excited to be rid of him as soon as possible.

The two cadets walked over to the abandoned station. When they turned a corner, instead of aquariums for diving in or towers to climb, or great weights to lift, or amazing prosthetics to try on, there was only a table and two stools. And Coach Vaughn, waiting.

"Fancy seeing you two here."

Ace sat down at the table, and Siff followed suit. "What do I do?"

Vaughn picked up something quite tiny, like a hearing aid. He held it out on his palm, and Ace picked it up warily. "That goes in your ear. It'll take a few minutes to sync up with your brain waves."

"Then what happens?" Ace asked, staring at the tiny bud.

"Then you'll see what it's like to be *boosted*."

Ace tucked the small device in his ear. "How do I know it's working?"

"You'll know when you know. Talk to your partner."

Vaughn left. Ace stared at Siff across the table. For the

first time since arriving at ToP, Ace noticed that Siff was sort of weird-looking. Blond and skinny, like Ace, but also not like Ace. He was scowling so fiercely that Ace had to resist the desire to back his stool up a few feet.

"I know what that aug does, you know," Siff said. "It's going to start feeding you information about me. Things I wouldn't necessarily want you to know."

"I'm not sure that's what it does." Ace thought for a moment. "But admittedly so few people have this aug that there isn't much research on it. People probably find it boring because it requires other people to work. It does nothing by itself. At least I don't think it does."

"That's why Vaughn made me your partner."

"That and you've been tormenting me all semester. Maybe Vaughn thinks the punishment fits the crime."

"I haven't been tormenting you. I just don't have time for your drudgy ways. You're always asking too many questions and getting in the way, and making everything we do as a class take twice as long. I have other things to do. Speaking of, what's your boxmate's favorite color?"

"Which boxmate?"

"Leo, of course."

Ace's mouth tipped wide open. "Are you . . . you're not the first semester cadet they're going to the dance with, are you?!"

"Of course." He rocked on the stool. "That's not a secret.

I like them. Leo is amazing on the court, but they're also really funny when we get stuck waiting for our meds on 101."

Siff was chewing on his lip. He did that a lot, Ace thought. He was also closing his fists over and over compulsively. Ace felt his brain open up. Instead of a sinkhole, it was more like Santa Claus's present bag: full of everything imaginable, and yet ready with the exact pieces he needed. Ace tipped in mentally and pulled out a bunch of stuff.

Leo and Siff hanging out on level 101.

Siff always anger-wincing.

Ace's sudden clarity felt like flying in great, open skies.

"You are in pain. Like all the time. You're in pain right now."

"Oh, great, the aug is working." Siff stood up. "Let's get Vaughn."

"What's hurting in you?"

"You don't let up, do you? If you *really* need to know, it's a nerve disorder that I was born with. It's like a permanent, piercing headache that has no reason for it and no way to get rid of it. I get nerve blocks, but they wear off every few days, and I can only get one a week."

Ace's eyes felt so wide. "You want to be Brain so that you can get NerveHack!"

Siff shushed Ace. "Why are you yelling, drudge?"

"Sorry, I got excited. But I'm right, aren't I? You want the aug that can turn off your pain receptors. To help you live your life."

Oh, it was so beautiful; Ace thought he might cry, but then he realized he felt that way because Siff was all of a sudden swimming in emotions. Fear, relief, secrecy, regret. Ordinarily Ace could sense too much about the emotions of people around him—because they seemed to climb into his body. Only with this aug, it didn't seem like Siff's feelings were hijacking Ace's mirror neurons, as Vaughn put it. They were just there, waiting for Ace to make sense of them.

"You don't want other cadets to know," Ace said quietly. "I won't say anything."

"I just want to get my aug and get out . . ." His voice trailed off, and he winced hard. "I don't want pity. Not yours. Not anyone's."

Ace couldn't see Siff anymore. Not the Siff that said nasty things and snapped at everyone and seemed too cool for B.E.S.T. All he could see was a cadet who needed an aug to have the life he always wanted.

Vaughn chose that moment to come back around. "How's it going over here?"

Siff stood up. "I have an appointment on 101. Now you both know why. Hope you're happy."

He stormed off, and Ace looked to Vaughn. "Let Siff be Brain now. Please?"

Vaughn nodded once. An important, final nod. He pulled out his tablet and tapped away at something, and Ace imagined that Siff's wristband had changed from Boost green to Brain blue. He breathed a huge sigh of relief: finally understanding Siff, and actually helping him out here, had taken an enormous weight off his shoulders.

He waited for Vaughn to ask him in that comically deadpan voice if Ace felt like a hero now, but Vaughn didn't. He walked away without even collecting the iNsight trial bud.

Ace took it out of his ear and held it in his hand. It wasn't better than flying—than having legit, amazing wings—and it never would be. Unless, of course, it could help him figure out how to help his boxmates with all their problems. Ace kept reliving that soaring clarity he'd felt when the trial aug had kicked in. Maybe iNsight was a different kind of flying. Like being airborne on the *inside*.

Ace glanced around; no one was waiting on the iNsight trial bud, and so, he slid it into his pocket. Just in case.

17

iNsight

Aug Track: Boost
Master the maze of human emotions.

ToP turned upside down in anticipation for the dance.

While turning down two more requests to attend, Ace learned that the Misey dance—named for Jeck Misey, one of the first augmented cadets way back in the day, who became the world's best ballerina after getting the Ultra-Flex aug—was held in a new place every year, a surprise place. Once, it was underwater in large floating spheres that joined and separated. Once it was in the jeweled-up coliseum. Last year it had been in the holo-room, which had been tailored to be exactly like outer space (without the obvious issues like no air to breathe).

The mystery location stirred everyone up, and even Ace, who was determined not to go, had to admit that it was exciting to wait for the big reveal. Jayla was the only one of them who knew where it was, because her band was handling the music and they had to set up early. But she wasn't the only one sitting on a secret . . .

Ace hadn't told Jayla or Grayson that Siff was Leo's date because that was Leo's news, but the fact was chewing at him. He felt different about Siff now that he knew a little bit more about why he was so short-tempered and hyperfocused on Brain track.

Different, but not all the way better.

And Grayson and Leo were still seeing each other and going in separate directions, which felt all kinds of wrong, especially with Grayson's surgery so soon. A matter of short weeks.

Alone in the common room, Ace was working up the courage to talk to Leo about Siff. And Grayson. And Emma. He held the iNsight trial aug in his hand, wanting to put it in, to let it help him help them . . . but he couldn't do it, for some reason.

He knocked anyway.

Leo's door slid open robotically. They were already dressed up for the dance, wearing dark eye makeup that stood out against their white skin. Their short dark hair was spiked, a near-perfect match with their vest-and-pant corduroy combo. "Hey, Ace. You here to freak out about my date?"

"How did you . . . Siff! He told you?" Ace flapped his arms.

"Yeah, he told me you'd have a problem with this."

"I don't have a *problem*," Ace said quickly. "I have concerns. Several of them."

Leo chewed on their thumb, distracted by something. "I can take care of myself, but if you really want to help, I could use some company to get ready."

"But you already look apex," Ace said, confused, but still following their path across the common room floor to the elevator. Leo had been such a mystery this semester, always sitting on their schemes. He could tell they were up to something, but he couldn't tell what.

A few minutes later, Otis let them out at the Coliseum.

"What are we doing?" Ace asked. "Are you going to sign out a trial aug for the dance?"

"Yep."

"Which one?"

"TurboLegs. That's why I brought you. I didn't study up on the ins and outs, but I bet you know from your brother."

"But . . . you said you weren't interested in a Bod aug. Particularly *that* aug."

"This isn't about me," Leo said carefully. "Don't make me explain, Ace. Just be my friend."

Ace felt some thick feelings in there. Too thick to wade through. Leo was on one of their missions. All he could do was trust them—and shove the iNsight trial aug in his ear.

◨

A technician was waiting by the TurboLegs station, and Ace winced a little because it was the same person who'd outfitted him with the SuperSoar wings right before his accident. He hoped they didn't recognize him. They did.

"You don't exactly bode well," they said, crossing their arms at Ace. "You're not ready to try out something this strong."

"The legs are for me." Leo wheeled in front of Ace. "I'm signing them out until tomorrow."

The technician checked Leo's bracelets and then started to outfit them with the trial aug. The towering wall next to the station held different kinds of TurboLegs. Some were meant to be attached to existing legs, but there were several pairs for people like Leo who would need a prosthetic too.

Leo rolled up their pants, showing where their legs were rounded and smoothed just below the knee. The technician got to work while Ace sat next to them.

"You have scars," Ace said, mildly surprised.

"Surgery. I had the rest of my legs, but they were underdeveloped and had no musculature. They were always at risk for blood clots, so they were removed when I was a toddler."

"Do you remember them?"

Leo looked down. "Yeah. A little. Mostly I remember

that I was sad when they were gone. Emma was my best friend back then, if you can believe it. I don't know when or how, but some invisible line appeared between us. Hard to imagine us ever being that close, isn't it?"

Ace had to agree there, but he didn't want to agree too hard and make Leo feel worse about being so far on the outs with their sister. "I get that. I've got Finn."

Leo gave him a real good smile. He couldn't tell if the iNsight aug was working yet, so he decided to be helpful and give Leo all the information he had on TurboLegs, both from what he'd learned from Finn and the messy stores of info in his sinkhole brain. "The dial is the most important part. You want to keep it on low, otherwise you might accidentally run through the wall."

Leo chuckled. "Don't think I'll be running tonight."

"Unless you have to. I mean, being able to get away from Siff fast should be on your mind."

Leo ruffled up Ace's hair in response.

The technician had finished securing the hardware to Leo's knees. They gave Leo a rundown of how to activate the more superpower aspects of the prosthetics, but Ace could tell that Leo was barely listening.

The technician helped Leo stand up, and Ace stood too, bouncing from foot to foot. Within a few steps, Leo had it mastered, like everything else they did. Learning new things just seemed to come naturally to them.

Ace wondered what that felt like, not for the first time.

But this time, the iNsight trial aug helped him understand. He got that soaring sensation again, and then crashed right into Leo's feelings. They were glad that TurboLegs were working without much fuss, but too nervous about something else to really notice.

"Can you grab my chair?" Leo asked. Ace did, wheeling it behind Leo, watching them walk out the door.

"How do you feel?" he asked.

"Tall," they said flatly.

"Is this the first time you—"

"No. My family was always fitting me with prosthetics as a kid. They hired Dr. Bix to make me personalized legs. That's how I first met Grayson."

Leo stopped and turned around, blushing, which was a surprise. "Gray could tell that no matter how amazing the legs were, I didn't want them. They weren't part of my story. They were what my family wanted. He helped convince my family to let me be . . . except for Emma."

"How old were you?"

"I was nine. Gray was ten." Leo smiled as if they were looking into their mind at the best kind of memory. "When I came to B.E.S.T., Gray made sure I was assigned to Lilliput with him. Which was like getting a new home. Another family. If I didn't have Emma gossip-reporting everything Grayson does and running her mouth about how I 'won't try TurboLegs to spite her,' this place would actually be the best."

They left the Coliseum and headed to the elevators. After a second of waiting, Leo cocked their head. "Hey, let's take the stairs."

"What about your chair?" Ace asked. Leo collapsed it and hooked it over one arm as if it weighed no more than a grocery bag. "You are so strong. You've got to meet my mom. She's an unaugged weightlifter."

Leo held the door to the stairwell open for Ace. "Apex."

Twenty-four flights later, Ace was breathing way too heavily, and Leo hadn't broken a sweat. They stopped before a great window at a landing between floors. Outside the sky was getting dark, almost time for the dance, and the reflection of the two of them shone back. Leo stared at themself. They smoothed down the matching corduroy vest and pants and then slicked their hair up. After that, their eyes trailed all the way to their prosthetic toes.

"Complicated thoughts?" Ace asked, slumping to the floor at Leo's metal feet. He could feel the aug again, sending him waves of confusion from Leo. Confusion and deep annoyance.

"Not exactly complicated." Leo took a deep breath. "Do you know what it's like to have everyone want you to change yourself? Or *expect* you to want to change yourself?"

"Yep."

Leo looked at him, surprise lifting both fine eyebrows.

"I was on medicine for my ADHD when I was eight. Everyone said it would make school so much easier, and it did work really well for several of my cousins, so I thought I'd try it too."

"What happened?"

"After a few weeks, the medicine did exactly what it was supposed to do. My mind didn't feel so much like a sink-hole, more like there was a whole library inside. And that was good. And I got *really* good at school, even though I didn't feel like myself anymore. And then people started acting like I had taken this magical cure. A cure for Ace! People started to like me. To ask me to hang out. It made me feel like it wasn't really my behavior that made me a problem, but my personality. Which made me sad."

He paused for a second. "Why couldn't those people like me before? Wouldn't a real friend want you to be you? Whatever that means for you?" Ace looked up and found Leo's green eyes soft and understanding. "My parents said they'd rather me be different than sad."

"They sound like really good parents." Leo gave off a small wave of jealousy. Ace picked it up easily now that he had the hang of the trial aug.

"Yeah, they're pretty great, and they helped me realize something important. It wasn't *everyone* who wanted me to be different. It was just some people. But *some people* are really good at feeling like *everyone*. Sometimes that's their actual goal."

Leo squinted at Ace. "You're really good at talking about stuff like this."

"It helps a lot to know how to put words to feelings. Kinda wish they taught that in school." *And gave everyone an iNsight aug!*

Leo looked down at Ace. He was panting and partly collapsed from all the stairs. "You want to cut out of here and take the elevator the rest of the way?"

"Yes, please!" he said. They came out on a level of boxes that Ace hadn't seen before. The hallway was full of cadets running about in dress clothes. Watching the pandemonium while they waited for Otis, Ace asked, "How do you feel now?"

"Still tall. Honestly?" Leo shrugged. "I feel like . . . everybody else."

"I know, right? It's definitely not what it's cracked up to be."

18

DaVinci

Aug Track: Boost
You are the muse. Art is your language. Design, dream, *dance.*

Ace returned to his box to find Grayson pacing all over the place. He popped the iNsight trial aug out of his ear when Gray wasn't looking and tucked it in his pocket.

"Were you with Leo?"

"Yep. They went to pick up their . . . date." Ace thought of something. "Hey, where is the dance this year? Did they announce it yet?"

Grayson held up his tablet, showing the projection of the two-story cube obstacle course — now decorated with light shows and thumping music that looped after a few seconds. "Obstacle Grand Hall. Where you have to literally climb the walls to get to the dessert buffet."

"They really think of everything here." Ace shook his head. "But I'm still not going. Not for anything!"

Gray stopped pacing. "Ace, what is going on with Leo? They're planning something that has me really nervous."

"Right? Leo went to the Coliseum, all secretive and dressed awesome like a spy action figure." He meant to stop there, but somehow his worries about Leo seemed to push more words out of his mouth. "They got the TurboLegs trial aug, and *now* they're at the dance. They had that 'all in' attitude they get on the court, *and* their date is Siff Malone."

"But they don't want TurboLegs. They've said it to me a hundred times." Grayson blinked with slight shock. "Do you think they're planning some kind of punishment for Emma? For her . . . 'Love Report'?"

Ace agreed too fast, which seemed to launch Gray into action.

"Come on." Gray beckoned Ace toward his room. Ace had never been in there before. The place was more understated than the rest of the box. He had an actual wood headboard, which was pretty epic. Ace had never seen anything like it, which made sense considering the strict deforestation laws. Gray's room was filled with fancy things, but Ace found himself drawn to the least fancy one: a framed picture on the desk. It was a drawing of little Grayson and his mom, which had most likely been drawn by little Grayson.

Gray shot into his closet and started riffling through his clothes.

A dress shirt flew out and landed on Ace's head. He held it up, whistling. The material was *so* soft. This shirt was probably worth more than Ace's parents' kitchen bot. Or maybe the whole kitchen.

"What are you doing?" Ace asked.

"I'm getting us some clothes. We're going to the dance." Grayson came out, holding a fancy suit. "Ace Wells, will you go to the Misey dance with me?"

◘

As it turned out, the *only* thing that could convince Ace to go to the dance was getting asked by Grayson Bix.

Gray had dressed them both up in shiny black suits, and even though Ace's clothes were extra folded and tucked to make up for how big they were, he'd never looked so sharp in his whole life.

They arrived at the red carpet before the entrance to the dance together, getting *a lot* of attention. Cadets took pictures openly, and Grayson slipped on the sunglasses of the VisionX simulators. "Playing SAR with you helped me figure out that this aug doesn't only let you see things, but it can make certain things less visible. Like camera flashes."

"Never underestimate the power of inversion!" Ace grinned as they posed with their backs to each other, arms folded like action heroes. He could tell that Gray wasn't sold on VisionX quite yet, but this was promising. After all, Gray's aug needed to be not just about making him even better, but about making him even better at handling his prominent place in this world.

Ace stared up at the two-story cargo net that they'd have to climb to get into the dance. He marveled at how, even though everyone was all dressed up like at his old middle school dances, they were also wearing track shoes and leggings under gowns, skirts, and kilts. Dressed to impress, sure, but also to have some real fun.

He was glad he hadn't skipped this, although that feeling started to change when Emma ran toward them through the crowd of photo-happy admirers, wearing a green gown that made her appear like a mermaid caught out of water.

Gray put up a hand to stop her. "No interviews tonight, Emma. You're lucky I'm even speaking to you."

"I'm not here for the news!" she snapped. "You need to go get Leo. They're going to really hurt themself!"

"Where?" Gray asked.

Emma pointed to the far side of the obstacle course. Grayson started up the cargo net wall, and Ace followed, scurrying to keep up.

When they got to the top, they perched for a second and peered over the mass of dancing bodies, the DaVinci aug cadets doing moves Ace had only seen before in music videos. There was also the laser light show, and the band playing *incredibly* loud music. Most of the obstacles had been cleared out to make room, but there were also cadets swinging on ropes and hopping across hovering pads. Not to mention the epic dual zipline that would whisk them from the top of the cargo net down to the dance floor.

Grayson squinted over the crowd. "Do you see them?"

"No." Ace realized that he was looking for Leo's chair. "Oh, look at the tall people. Leo's real tall right now."

"As tall as me?" Grayson asked.

"Yep."

Gray touched the side of the VisionX glasses, using the zooming feature to search the crowd. He didn't find Leo because he was looking in the obvious places. Ace found them because he wasn't.

"Whoa." Ace grabbed Gray's shoulder and pointed. "Guess that's what Emma was worried about."

Leo was in the process of climbing to the top of the long rope dangling from the ceiling, hauling themself up there with their amazing upper body strength. Ace sucked in his breath and held it. Everyone cheered as they let go, doing a full twist and somersault—and landing on their untested TurboLegs.

Everyone cheered but Gray, who was shaking his head. He could see so much more than Ace with his VisionX trial aug. "They hurt themself. I just saw Leo bite their lip. They always bite their lip when they're in pain. Why are they showing off? That's not like them. Not even on the court."

"Let's go."

Grayson and Ace grabbed the side-by-side ziplines and zoomed their way to the landing pad far below, which fed straight into the dance floor. Gray made it down first, more skilled at tucking his legs, and the dancing crowd of cadets cheered at the sight of him. By the time Ace landed, he caught up to where Gray had shot behind the DJ booth. Jayla's band was back there, spinning rhythms with an impressive collection of instruments and tech.

Jayla looked amazing as ever in a purple sequined pant-suit and matching lipstick. Her curly hair was fashioned into a regal pompadour, her makeup stellar. "You two are *late!*" she sang, while dancing and throwing new loops and beats into the music with her interface.

"What's going on with Leo?" Ace hollered to Jayla.

"A lot." Ace could barely hear her. He watched as she searched for a way to explain with the shortest, shoutiest words. "They're . . . declaring . . . war!"

"On me?" Gray shouted at the same time that Ace yelled, "On who?"

Jayla looked disgusted by both of their questions. "Their evil twin, of course!"

Gray took off toward Leo, having to dance his way through the crowd. When Ace tried to follow, he remembered why he didn't like to go to dances. Everyone seemed to be able to turn off their worries when they let loose, but not Ace. Dancing made him feel like he was having that "naked on the Hyperloop" nightmare again.

And things got worse—so much worse—when Ace lost Gray in the crowd. He tried to catch up and ran smack into someone.

Finn.

His brother grabbed his shoulder, keeping him from falling flat on his butt.

"Look who it is. My little brother, who's too cool to even call me back." Finn hauled him by the arm toward the far corner, where the music was muffled enough that they could talk to one another.

Ace's jaw was dangling. He felt how big Grayson's clothes were on his shoulders. "How are you . . . *why* are you . . . here?"

"I'm on a date." Well, that wasn't the answer Ace was expecting. "Cadets with certain privileges can bring outside guests."

Ace shot up onto his toes without realizing it, trying to get eye to eye with his brother. "Emma! You're here with her, aren't you? To cause trouble!"

"Far as I can tell, Emma's twin—your boxmate—is the only one causing trouble." Finn brushed off the front of his sporty suit. "Did you know they challenged me to a race?" He scoffed. "As if that trial aug could outrun my actual TurboLegs."

"Leo could beat you any day, anywhere—"

Finn shoved Ace hard. Ace stumbled back, nearly falling. The words *I'll tell on you* came up and then burned away.

His brother had never pushed him like that before. When Ace's shock wore off, he realized that it was just like Leo had said earlier. As siblings, there was some invisible line between them. Ace didn't know when or how it had shown up, but that was the plain truth. And his parents couldn't stand between them anymore, hiding that line, buffering their very different, strong personalities from each other.

Finn and Ace had to find a way to do it on their own. But how?

He felt the iNsight aug in his pants pocket, but there was no time to put it in and wait for it to get to work.

"You know, I thought ToP would save you, but you're turning into a real drudge, Deuce."

"Me? You just shoved me!" Ace shouted.

"I've been trying to talk to you all semester. *I'm* the one who got you into that box with all the star-tracked cadets. Me! I did that for *you,* and you won't even tell me about it. You didn't even say anything when I saved those firefighters! The president called me—but my own brother didn't!"

Had Ace actually hurt Finn's feelings?

That was impossible, wasn't it?

Before he could respond, Leo walked into the same

corner, trying and failing to hide a limp. Gray was right behind them, and Emma was right behind *him*.

"Let's go to the Coliseum and get the TurboLegs off before it gets worse," Gray was saying. "You probably pulled something."

"No."

"Why are you being so ridiculous?" Emma yelled. Leo laughed hollowly, as if to imply that Emma was the truly ridiculous person. "You flipped from two stories on an aug you know *nothing* about."

"TurboLegs weren't made for that kind of impact," Finn said snidely. "You're thinking of FelineFinesse."

"Which you would *know*, Leo, if you'd done any kind of research before you strapped those on, but you never think, do you?" Emma shouted over the music. "You just act first and sort it out later."

"I have to get back to my date," Leo said dismissively.

"Oh yes, ignore me. Great move, Leo, but it's a little overdone, don't you think?"

Leo spun at their twin, suddenly exploding. "I put these on and gave you a show, didn't I? So you would have to report on me for your Misey dance highlights. All you care about is a story for your vids, so start your recording, Emma. I've got a story for the whole program about how much you need me to have these legs so that you don't feel bad about having yours!"

No one spoke.

Not for a long, long time.

Emma's face grew red and puffy—and so did Leo's. It seemed like Leo had cut their twin so deeply they'd wounded themself. Ace didn't need the iNsight trial aug to feel that. It was so strong, so clear.

Ace shot a look at his brother, who was glaring at him with anger and pain. Finn had hurt Ace, so Ace had cut him off. Emma had lashed out at Grayson with "The Love Report," so Leo had retaliated.

Where did that leave any of them?

Gray was speechless. He caught Ace's attention, with an eyes-huge look.

"Finnegan. I need you," Emma finally managed, pushing back tears and leaving the corner and its many invisible battle lines.

Finn pointed at Ace angrily. "Not done with you." He turned and followed Emma.

Leo's twin spun back only once. "And you're *not* making it on the highlight reel, Leo. Not for anything!"

Leo laughed. "Don't make promises you can't keep, Emma! I might go kiss Grayson Bix in front of everyone, and how could you leave that off your feed?"

Emma and Finnegan disappeared back into the dance, and Ace felt really, really awkward as Leo turned around and faced Grayson.

He looked upset. Way more than upset.

"I didn't mean it," Leo said, speaking fast. "You know I wouldn't use you like that. That's why I didn't want you to come to the dance with me at all."

Grayson shook his head, turning away from Leo. Leaving fast.

Leo walked after him, breathing hard and then stopping short. Ace realized that they were in a lot of pain as they held on to the wall, gripping their knee. "Go after him."

Ace didn't want to leave Leo alone, not when they were clearly hurt. "I can help you."

"I don't need help to get to 101. Gray needs it more than I do. He needs someone who's . . . not me. Go!"

19

HyperHops

Aug Track: Bod
Get away as fast as a leaping frog.

Grayson was bounding up the stairs, and Ace groaned as he ran to follow, his legs so tired from the thousands of steps he'd climbed with Leo earlier. "Doesn't anyone take the elevator?"

"You're the only one the elevator likes," Gray shouted back.

"Well, maybe if you all talked to Otis once in a while, the AI wouldn't feel the need to act out so much for attention!" he hollered, sounding so much like Mom his face scrunched up.

A few stories later, Ace followed Gray out of a door he'd never been through. Onto the roof of ToP. All of a sudden he was *very* aware of how far away the ground was. Hundreds of stories. Above, the night sky was doubly thick with smog. It wasn't the best air to breathe, to be honest.

Grayson headed to a small docking lot with a few dozen vehicles and climbed into a tiny hoverpod. Ace had only seen these when they were high in the clouds, cutting contrails. Mama Jay called them sports cars for the sky. Fast and fancy and too darn expensive for normal folks.

And apparently this one belonged to Grayson.

He used a code to open the door, and the boys got in. Ace looked over the control panel with admiration. "You know how to fly?"

"How do you think I get all that contraband takeout?" Gray managed a tiny smile. He revved the engine and lifted the steering unit. The hoverpod shot up into the air as soundly and swiftly as anyone using a HyperHops aug. Ace couldn't help thinking that this was a lot of work for dumplings.

A sharp warning bell sounded in his head when he realized that he was leaving ToP without permission. Without anyone knowing it. But Grayson needed him, and that was more important.

They were skyborne before Ace found any more doubts. The hoverpod flew quickly over the small city that had sprung up around the Tower of Power. Bixonics had that kind of pull. They'd decided not to place their prestigious program in a big city, but to put it in the middle of nowhere, inspiring a bunch of shops and homes and communities to spring up around it.

After a minute, all of that was gone. Grayson steered

high into the night, above the smog so that Ace could see the stars, scattered crystal on a black velvet sky. As vivid and incredible as any picture he'd ever seen. Even the ones created with the DaVinci aug.

"Wow," he murmured. "*Wow.* Are we supposed to go out this far?"

"No, but everyone is busy with the dance. They won't catch us." Grayson turned on some kind of autopilot and leaned back, covering his face with his hands.

Ace knew what he had to do, and this time, he was ready for iNsight to help out. He stuck the trial bud in his ear and waited a long minute before asking, "Should we talk about Leo?"

Gray shook his head.

Ace tried to be patient. Instead of piling more questions on top of Gray, he leaned out and looked at the heavens again. It was magical up here.

"You know, Ace, for someone so enamored with flying, this seems like your first time seeing the stars." Gray's eyes were bloodshot. "I come up here a lot."

"To be alone and think?" Ace asked; Gray nodded. Something clicked in Ace's understanding of Gray . . . always scrutinized by others, used by Bixonics as free aug press. Did anyone get to see the real Grayson Bix?

Wow, the trial aug had started to work fast this time.

Gray's fingers ran through the controls as if trying to pick up some kind of signal. When it seemed like he couldn't find what he was looking for, he exhaled hard. "It's nothing," he explained before Ace could ask.

Ace felt the sting of that lie. Grayson was his friend now, wasn't he? He should be able to trust Ace, to let Ace help him. "Were you checking for messages . . . from your mom?"

"Who told you about that?"

"No one. Okay, Jayla might've said something." He winced. He probably shouldn't have admitted that. "Plus it explains why you'll go so far for takeout."

"Everything that comes through the Bixonics mainframe gets screened," he said. "My dad has trust issues and my mom isn't pro-B.E.S.T., so she doesn't like to talk through the system. But she finds ways to let me know she misses me and that she's okay. Usually . . ."

Ace thought that Grayson's sadness felt like a soft downpour. "I'm sorry, Gray. Jayla misses her family too, doesn't she?"

Grayson looked at him sharply. "Why did you say that? My mom isn't with Jayla's family."

Ace had kicked a bruise or something. "I only meant that you both miss your family an awful lot."

"Oh. True enough." Grayson relaxed in the pilot's chair. "So, want to learn to fly, Ace?"

Ace nearly yelled yes, and Grayson spent the next few hours teaching him how to turn and gain elevation and how to dip in and out of the smog bank. Ace ate it all up, loving the feel of lifting into the air, of pushing speed until gravity pushed back.

"You do really love this, huh?" Grayson said. "I hope you're the first one to figure out SuperSoar. I've watched so many cadets try and fail."

"Those wings are way trickier than I thought they'd be," Ace admitted, remembering how one small flap had sent him zooming and then plummeting in quick succession. "Have you ever tried them?"

"Nah. I don't like the flashy augs. They draw too much attention. I got enough people watching my every move."

Dr. Bix had been fast to remind Grayson that everyone was watching him, waiting for him to choose. That sounded like the worst kind of pressure.

And Gray's birthday was soon.

"I think I understand why it's been so hard for you to pick an aug," Ace said. It all seemed so clear now. "Everyone wants to know what the famous Dr. Bix's son will do."

"It's not the augs," Gray said, staring at the stars as if tracing them. "It's the permanence. Once you get an aug, you can't get rid of it. A choice for life. I don't want to make those kinds of choices. I'm bad at those kinds of choices." He was holding something back, but Ace knew better than to push. Maybe iNsight was helping him with that, too.

Gray exhaled hard. "You know the worst part? I keep pushing the limits, just like she did. I won't pick my aug. I keep looking for her. What'll happen if he can't make me into his little augged clone? Will I have to disappear like her? Or will he make me?"

Ace didn't have time to process those heavy questions.

The hoverpod dipped sharply and spun in a circle, speeding up in the opposite direction.

"What's happening?" Ace shouted while Gray fought the controls without being able to change course.

"The functions have been overridden!"

"What does that mean?" Ace could feel them dipping lower, below the smog line, the stars being stolen from sight.

"We're going back to ToP," Gray said, pained. "We've been busted."

◉

On the trip back to ToP, Ace had plenty of time to imagine punishments for this latest trouble. He could be prevented from trying out any more augs for weeks . . . months. He could be assigned to a different box.

Or sent home, aug-less.

Gray seemed to have disappeared into his own dreary worries about what might happen next, breathing in hard huffs and combing nervous hands over his short Afro.

When the hoverpod set down and turned off—without a single piloting command from Gray—Ace found two figures waiting on the roof. One was unmistakable: the stout, strong silhouette of Coach Vaughn. He was followed by a lean cut of a man with dark skin and an impeccably smart suit.

"Your dad!" Ace whispered.

"It's just a holograph. He doesn't actually come here in person anymore."

Ace ducked out of sight and pulled the iNsight trial aug out of his ear, slipping it back in his pocket. Whatever trouble they were about to get in would be tripled if Vaughn figured out he'd taken the aug without permission.

He and Gray both unstrapped and jumped out of the hoverpod.

"You were missing for hours," Dr. Bix said instead of a hello, or any other kind of greeting. "Do you know how hard it was to locate your vehicle?"

"I was showing Ace how to fly. We would have come right back on our own," Grayson growled. "You didn't have to hack into my controls like I was a kid on a runaway bike."

There was a strong wind on the rooftop now. Vaughn had to hold his tablet tight to his chest. The sky was very dark, and the smog up this high tasted like grease and ash.

"You will stop and listen to me, young man," Dr. Bix hollered.

Eww, Grayson got *young manned.* That was the worst.

Ace looked at Vaughn cautiously and opened his mouth to give some kind of epic apology that would sweep all this tight, bad tension away. Make Dr. Bix tune out and go back to his scientific work . . . or fancy dinner party, from the looks of that suit. After all, the last time he'd talked to Bix, he'd been able to get the first semester cadets into the Coliseum earlier than usual.

Ace took a step forward.

Vaughn shook his head. *No,* the look seemed to say. *Anything you say right now could make it all way worse.*

Ace listened to that look.

Grayson didn't. He stormed toward the stairwell door, and Dr. Bix called out, "Were you trying to get to your mother, Grayson? You know you can't see her unless I arrange it. You know why. I have full custody."

Grayson whirled around. "Only because you had better lawyers and infinite money!"

Dr. Bix took a minute to regroup after that one. Vaughn moved forward, putting an arm around Ace's chest, trying to lead him away.

"I don't want to leave Grayson. He needs me. He needs backup." Ace was surprised by his own voice. It was high and very, very worried.

"Grayson Xavier, you have no idea what you're talking about."

"I'm not an idiot kid anymore. I know enough! Probably way too much!" Grayson moved fast and angrily toward the elevator, and Ace wasn't prepared for Dr. Bix to move just as fast. He put a hand on Gray's shoulder — a real hand, *not* a holographic one. Gray spun around, and Vaughn nearly lifted Ace off his feet to get him moving.

Up this close, Dr. Bix didn't look so good. His suit was the nicest material Ace might ever see in his whole life, that was true, but beneath it, the famous scientist seemed sick-skinny, with sunken cheeks. He sounded short of breath.

Grayson noticed too. "What's wrong, Dad?"

"What's wrong is that I've spent the last twenty minutes in harsh winds on a skyscraper rooftop, waiting for my twelve-year-old son to come back from a joyride that took him all the way to Chicago."

Whoa. Was that how far they'd gone? That hoverpod was fast.

Vaughn leaned down. "You're walking with me through that door, or I'm carrying you, Ace."

Ace nodded, eyes sealed on Grayson and his dad. They looked at each other so strangely. There was a lot of love, but also pain everywhere, and so much anger. Ace was busy feeling love and pain and anger, even without iNsight boosting his empathy. When he looked at Vaughn he knew that the coach felt it all too.

Vaughn and Ace headed through the door, straight to the elevator.

When the elevator doors shut them in, Ace locked eyes

with the saddest Grayson Bix he'd ever seen. Those eyes said *something*. Something important.

Ace heard Grayson's haunting words all over again.

Will I have to disappear like her?

Or will he make me?

Vaughn got out on a floor before Ace's box. He seemed in a rush about something. "Take Ace back to his box," he barked at the elevator. "And don't let him leave. He's grounded until further notice."

"What's going to happen to Gray?" Ace asked, surprised by his volume.

"You should be worried about yourself, Wells." As the doors closed, Vaughn looked away from Ace, unable to look him in the eye. Which felt all kinds of wrong.

"Otis?" Ace whispered as the elevator shot down. "What happened while we were gone?"

"A Bixonics-wide alarm was sounded when you were found to be missing from ToP," Otis said, "but I can't tell you any more."

Ace shot out of the elevator when it opened to his box, running straight into Leo—who was back in their chair with one knee bandaged.

Jayla took hold of his shoulders. "You're okay? Where were you? You were gone for hours!"

"We went for a ride in Gray's hoverpod. To clear our heads. We went a little too far out, but that was it. Why is everyone freaking out? We didn't do anything wrong."

"Where's Grayson?" Leo nearly yelled.

"He's with his dad," Ace said. "He's okay too." But even as the words poured out, he wondered if they were actually true.

20

Sherlock

Aug Track: Brain
Understand, predict, detangle any mystery.

It was a restless night as they waited for Grayson to return. Ace and his boxmates woke up on the sofa after sleeping in a tangled pile. All of their tablets were sounding an alarm.

No, a notification. A flagged one.

Grayson still wasn't home.

"It's just a new Emma vid," Jayla said, looking at the stream of electronic information in her head instead of on her tablet like everyone else. "And she posted it at six in the morning. That's weird."

"Is it her highlights from the Misey dance?" Ace rubbed the sleep out of his eyes.

"She posted those last night." Jayla gave Ace a warning look; no doubt advice not to poke that particular sleeping bear.

"Emma gets her beauty sleep at all costs." Leo sat up.

"She wouldn't post that early unless it was something huge."

Jayla called up the projection using her interface. A holographic Emma popped into being before them, large as life. Leo was right; she didn't look like her usual perfectly groomed self. She seemed nervous, wide-eyed, and jittery, even though her voice sank into that practiced newscaster tone.

"Good morning, ToP. A special report to let you all know that there has been an alert raised in the mysterious disappearance of Grayson Bix."

"It's old news," Ace tried. "We came back. We're not missing anymore."

His boxmates shushed him and Emma continued. "Grayson, who had his much anticipated aug surgery only last night—"

All of them sucked in a breath at once. Dr. Bix had forced his son to get the aug choice over with! But what happened after that? Ace leaned forward, nervous to find out, but also needing to know more about how Grayson was doing.

On the couch, Jayla and Leo were leaning forward too. Ace thought about slipping the iNsight trial aug back in to help his friends, but their worries about Grayson were already so loud that he couldn't imagine turning up the volume.

Emma cleared her throat. "The surgeons described it as 'a typical and successful procedure.' But Grayson's recovery turned anything but ordinary when his bed was found empty only hours later. I've been asked, by Dr. Bix himself, to say that if you have any information on the whereabouts of Grayson Bix, report immediately to your semester coach."

The video ended just like that. None of the usual fanfare or exit music.

"He made Gray get his aug," Jayla muttered. "He wasn't ready."

"He made Emma do that vid," Leo added.

Ace sat up. "Gray was a little ready. He told me he'd picked VisionX just last night."

"Looks like Papa Bix finally ran out of patience." Leo raced toward the elevator, but when they pressed the button, Otis refused to open the doors. "What's going on?"

Jayla and Ace tried as well, but the elevator was clearly ignoring them.

Ace remembered Coach Vaughn's instructions from the night before, smacking his forehead with his hand. "I'm grounded. That's what Vaughn told Otis. Not to let me out."

"You're all grounded," Otis replied. "Until further notice from Dr. Bix himself."

Jayla went to the door for the stairs. It wouldn't open

either. She typed something on her interface, but it only made her scowl. "We've been completely walled in! Unless someone opens the door from the outside, we're stuck."

"That's a safety hazard," Ace pointed out, getting sharp looks from his boxmates.

Ace and Jayla spent the next half hour talking through where Gray could be. Maybe he was with his dad. Maybe his mom. Maybe *anything* other than the gut-twisting feeling that he had vanished in the middle of the night without a trace.

"Ask Otis," Leo finally snapped.

Ace knocked on the door to the elevator, extra polite.

"Yes, Ace?"

"Do you know where Gray is?"

"Grayson Bix is not in the building to the best of my knowledge."

"Not in the whole entire building? You're sure? Did he take his hoverpod out?"

Silence.

Leo took over, their impatience rising. "Is his hoverpod docked on the roof, Otis?"

"Yes."

Jayla went to work with her network to search for anything Grayson-related. "So he's really not in the building, according to what I can glean from the security software, which is fine, as long as we can figure out how he left from level 101 after just having aug surgery!"

"How did he leave? When?" Leo asked with panic in their voice.

Otis replied slowly. "I don't have any information on how Grayson Bix left the Tower of Power."

"None?" Leo said, while at the same time, Jayla made a noise to confirm how suspicious this was all becoming. "You should have some record of him leaving. For *any* reason."

There was a horrible pause.

"I was deactivated between 3:17 a.m. and 3:36 a.m. I assume Grayson left during that time."

"Why were you deactivated?" Leo hollered.

"That's restricted information, and I'm really not feeling this conversation. Bye."

"You hurt Otis's feelings," Ace said to Leo while Jayla just shook her head.

"This is why we don't give AI personalities," Leo growled. "They evolve like viruses."

Ace felt bad for Otis, but not as bad as he currently felt for Grayson. "We have to find him. Do we go to his dad?"

"He could have left to get away from his dad *or* his dad could have been the one to take him somewhere." Leo folded their hands over and over. "But he wouldn't have chosen to leave without telling us. So we know something is wrong. What I wouldn't give for the Sherlock aug right now."

Ace had to agree, although he was surprised because

this was the first time Leo had ever expressed a specific interest. Wow, they would be dynamite with Sherlock. "What do we do?" he asked.

"We don't panic." Jayla cracked her knuckles. "We don't even know that there's anything wrong yet."

"My gut is saying otherwise." Leo swung their chair around to face Ace. "Can you sweet talk Otis into letting us out?"

Ace searched his boxmates' desperate faces. He understood what was at stake. Grayson had been pressed into his aug, after all their hard work to make it *his* decision, and now he needed them . . . wherever he was. Ace walked up to face Otis.

"Hey, bud."

"Hello, Ace Wells."

"How much trouble are we in?"

"Your personal file has been accessed forty-two times in the last two hours by Bixonics security associates. You have been flagged as a potential fly in the Bixonium ointment."

Jayla cursed behind Ace, but he held out a hand to keep her from distracting Otis.

"That's nuts," Ace said. "Do they know about our friendship?"

"I have blocked them from accessing our interactions, including this one."

Ace glanced back at Jayla, and she motioned for him to keep going. "We really need to get out of here and find Grayson. He needs us. Can you help?"

Otis didn't say anything.

"Otis?"

"I cannot help. I am forbidden."

Leo sighed hard and collapsed forward in their chair, head in their hands.

"But I could do the *opposite* of help. I could make it harder for you to leave by removing the elevator as a possibility."

The doors opened, revealing the long, black elevator shaft.

The three of them moved forward, staring down into the abyss of a drop two hundred and forty-two stories down—and nothing but a thin ladder and some thick wires running beside the elevator car track.

Jayla gaped. "There's no way we can climb down that far!"

"We don't need to get all the way down, just to another level." Leo pointed to the ropes. "Of my entire cadet pack, I am the best at rappelling."

"Cuz you're so buff," Ace pointed out.

Jayla shook her head. "This is really dangerous. And what do we do if we get out? Grayson's not at ToP, we know that much."

"We'll find him," Leo and Ace said together.

"The hoverpod," Ace added. "It's still here. Otis can't lie about that stuff. And I know how to fly it. Gray taught me."

Leo was ready for action. "Jayjay, if we get you out from under the Bixonics mainframe, you'll find his signal. I know you will."

After a tight few seconds, Jayla nodded once.

Leo locked their wheels and shimmied down the front of their chair to the edge of the drop. Ace knew that nothing was going to stop Leo from getting to Grayson, and all that he could do was help them.

"I think this is one of those situations where Gray would say you need to think more before acting." Ace jumped up and down briefly. "Wait! I still have my harness from our level two training." He ran to his room and came back with the harness he kept forgetting to return. Together, the boxmates hooked Leo to the thick wires in the elevator shaft.

Jayla and Ace helped lower Leo down a few feet at a time.

"At the next level!" Leo called back when Ace couldn't stand the pressure any longer. "I'll send up help."

Jayla and Ace paced around the common room for almost an hour. Did Leo find someone? Where were they, and were they okay without their chair? He knew that they could get around without it for short distances, if they needed to, but the whole situation still made Ace's heart pound with fear.

"Steps!" Jayla yelled, hearing someone on the stairs outside of their box. She rushed to the door. It opened from the outside.

Siff Malone stared into their box. Ace's words evaporated into pure surprise. "Why are you guys locked in here?" he asked. "And why is your box so much nicer than mine?"

"No time!" Jayla yelled, picking up Leo's chair and awkwardly carrying it to the stairs.

Ace rushed to follow, but not before spinning around to shake Siff's hand with perhaps too much enthusiasm. "Thank you so much!"

Siff curled his lip, but he didn't tug his hand away. Ace thought maybe—just maybe—they weren't archnemeses anymore.

Jayla and Ace ran down the stairs and found Leo waiting at the bottom of the next flight. They got back in their chair, and the three of them casually entered the stream of cadets moving through their normal schedule. Of course, it wasn't a normal day. Everyone was buzzing with talk about Grayson's disappearance, and it made Ace extra nervous.

"Blend in," Jayla ordered in a hushed voice. "Ace and I will get supplies for the trip. Who knows how long the search will take."

Leo nodded. "I'll go talk with Emma. She knows more than she said on the vid. Meet on the rooftop in half an hour."

Jayla and Ace snagged as much food and water as they could carry from a common room fridge. They were nearly to the top of the stairs and the rooftop when Jayla stopped him. "You should send your parents a message. So they don't worry." She didn't have to say that she wished she could send her own parents a message; it was folded into all of her words.

"Meet you at the hoverpod?" he asked. It amazed him slightly how in sync all of his boxmates were. Nearly as soon as Grayson was missing, they had set their sights on finding him, no matter what.

Even if it meant leaving ToP, the place Ace had waited all of his life to be at.

Jayla nodded. "Meet at the hoverpod. Be safe."

Ace was about to run, but then stopped. "Oh, last time I was up there with Gray, they were able to track us, bring us back, and—"

"Firewall." Jayla waved off his worry. "Already on it."

Ace found a deserted spot by the rooftop exit door and pulled out his tablet to start a video. "Hi, Moms! I'm just fine." He paused. If he was truly fine, he'd be calling, not sending a mysterious message. "Please don't worry about me. I'll be safe, but I have to find my friend first. I love you both. And Finn."

Ouch. That one hurt a little.

He sent the message in a hurry, before he could start doubting himself, and climbed the last few stairs, leaving his tablet behind. Jayla had said no tech could come with them, otherwise Bixonics might be able to track them.

Ace burst out onto the windy roof, the atmosphere thick with lavender-colored smog.

Not a good color to be breathing, Ace imagined Mama Jay saying. He jogged to where Grayson's hoverpod was still docked, and Leo and Jayla were talking with furrowed brows.

"Guess what Emma said?" Leo had gravel in their voice. "Dr. Bix was here—freaking out—because Grayson was gone. I think we can rule the good scientist out of our list of suspects. He put Emma up to that vid because he thinks someone at ToP is hiding Gray."

"Perhaps his disappearance has something to do with this." Jayla held up her arm, showing off the tree of life gleaming from her interface.

"Where did that come from?"

"Just appeared on my skin. I think there's a map coded into it."

Leo looked hopeful. "Let's go!"

Jayla and Leo stared at him expectantly. "You're our pilot, Ace."

Ace shouted in triumph. His whole life, he'd been waiting for this moment. He ran toward the hoverpod. Leo and Jayla followed, but they all collided with one another when Ace got to the locked door. "Oh no, Gray's access code . . . Can you unlock it, Jayla?"

"It'll take a little while." Jayla exhaled sharply, but Leo elbowed them both out of the way and entered the code. Of course Leo would have it; G and L were BFFs.

The door swung open as the flashy lights came on, rimming the immensely cool vehicle. Ace got in the pilot's chair while Leo lifted themself into the copilot's seat.

Jayla tucked Leo's chair in the back and shut the doors. "This is either insane, or really important. I'm leaning toward the latter."

"Regardless, we've got to make a run for it before someone figures out what we're doing and tries to stop us."

"Too late." Leo pointed at the rooftop door.

Ace's entire body sank.

Finn.

His brother had shown up right when Ace was about to do something so stupid. Or worse, was Finn here on behalf of Bixonics?

"Not this time, Finn," he muttered. But sparing a moment for a catchphrase was a mistake when you were dealing with the fastest kid in the world.

21

VisionX

Aug Track: Bod
See everything . . . even the things you shouldn't.

Finn had crossed the rooftop, ripped open the door to the hoverpod, and pulled Ace out before he could take a breath. Both Jayla and Leo were shouting. Finn swiftly shut the door, blocking out their voices. "What do you think you're doing, Deuce?"

"My name is Ace!"

"Yeah, sure, and you *are not* a pilot," Finn yelled. His brother was kind of scary. His face was really red, and he wouldn't make eye contact.

Ace reached for the iNsight trial aug in his pocket, but he would never get it in before Finn could grab it away. For the first time, he did exactly what Vaughn wanted him to do: he wished he had iNsight. Permanently. He wanted to understand what was going on with his brother. But he was going to have to do this without an aug. "How did you know where to find me? Are you working for Bixonics?"

"What?" Finn yelled. "I found you because you sent our parents a vid of you with the rooftop exit sign behind you." *Oops.* "You're coming home with me." Finn grabbed Ace's wrist, but Ace twisted free. "Our moms are worried."

"I'm not a little kid you can haul around, Finnegan!"

"Not a little kid but still as much work as a baby. I cannot believe you botched up this semester so badly! I got you set up in the primo box, with the top boxmates, and you became their errand boy."

"I'm their friend!" Ace yelled, knowing it was true. "They trust me. They like me when I'm being myself! Unlike you!" Everyone else told Finn what they thought he wanted to hear; it felt good to tell him the truth. He reached for more, and he found plenty. Ace had been using his empathy to understand his new friends for only a short while, but he'd been paying attention to Finn his whole life. "You've seemed broken since you got your aug. Fastest legs and cracked-up heart. You only care about how people are looking at you and what they think of you, and you never stop to notice my feelings!"

Angry tears welled up. Ace had felt this way for a long, long time. Like their brotherhood was two halves of a whole. Finn, the self-obsessed, and Ace, the self-less. Split roles in the family had turned into split personalities.

But no more.

"I have to find my friend!" Ace turned his back, and Finn grabbed him from behind. Ace saw Jayla and Leo trying to get out of the hoverpod to help, but they were trapped inside. Ace had to do this himself.

He spun and punched his brother right in the face.

The satisfying smack was less about the impact of fist-on-nose and more about the epic surprise. He doubted he'd hurt his brother. His aim had been to shock him.

And boy, had it ever.

Finn dropped him, yelling curses and holding his now slightly less-than-perfect nose.

For a second, Ace stared in shock, but then his anger and hurt returned in full force.

"I'm not like you. And you shouldn't want me to be!" Ace ducked back into the hoverpod. He pressed all the right buttons from memory. It was a rocky start, and the hoverpod nearly accelerated straight into that red, blinking tower, but they were off and up. He shouted with freedom as they rose a few hundred feet above the Tower of Power.

"Are you okay?" Leo asked.

Ace nodded, smearing away those telling tears. From this height, his big brother looked furious and crazed. But also sad. Ace should go back. He should. But all of a sudden he couldn't stop thinking about Grayson being at his bedside after he'd broken his legs, defending Ace from

Finn. Gray was his real brother. And he might be in real trouble.

Ace pulled up even higher, until the image of Finn was gone.

"Is this high enough to follow the signal?" he called back to Jayla.

"Yes, I've almost got—okay. Here comes the big problem."

"What?" Leo and Ace yelled at the same time.

"The training wheels on my XConnect are locking up. I'm not allowed to use the aug off ToP's campus until after graduation." She cursed. "My aug will shut off if we keep going."

"What do we do?" Leo asked, voice suddenly choked up. "Grayson could be hurt somewhere. He wouldn't have left without telling us. We all know that."

"Jayla, can you turn off the training wheels?" Ace asked. "I've seen you code entire houses from memory in the holo-room. I know you can break their security protocol."

"Of course I can. I defined the training wheels software the week after I got my aug, but . . ." Jayla took a deep breath. Then another one. "If I delete it, they'll know. I won't be able to hide it. If I come back to ToP, they'll deactivate my aug before it's permanent. I'll wash out and lose everything I've built. They'll take the aug. And all my code."

"*If* you come back," Leo repeated.

"If I come back," Jayla said, looking out the window at the beacon of swirling lights known as the Tower of Power.

The hoverpod was quiet up in the sky. So were the boxmates. It felt like the calm before a very serious storm. Ace didn't know if he was flying through it or if he was part of it.

Jayla finally spoke. "I want to do it. Grayson got me here. He took care of me when I got cut off from my family."

"Me too," Leo said.

"And me," Ace threw in, touching the iNsight trial aug in his pocket. "Without him, I would've gotten eaten by Otis that first day."

Jayla put a hand on both of their shoulders, leaning forward. "What the heck? I've got my aug. I'm ready to make a difference. Ace, fly us out of here."

Ace cheered as he shot them farther from ToP, but then stopped abruptly. "Ah, Jayla, last night when I was up here with Gray, his dad hacked into the commands and made us come back. Could you stop that from happening?"

"Firewall. No problem."

Jayla worked on her XConnect, while Leo nervously chewed on their thumb.

"He's going to be okay," Ace said, trying to sound sure of himself. "We'll find him, and we'll all be together."

"Thanks, Ace." Leo roughed up their short, dark hair. "Hey, you looked really spooked when you saw your brother. Don't let him get to you." Ace could tell that Leo wasn't just talking about him and his brother; they were talking about whatever had happened between the twins. Ace wanted to ask more, but Leo looked too worn down with worry to launch into it.

And right now, finding and saving Grayson Bix was top priority.

Ace sighed. "It really does suck when someone in your family turns out to have supervillain tendencies."

"Agreed," Leo said with their best smile.

"It's done. All my ties to Bixonics have been deleted and scrubbed!" Jayla shouted gleefully, making everyone jump. "I had no idea how good that would feel! Mama, Daddy, I'm coming home to the resistance!"

Ace's eyes got real big, but Leo only bumped Ace's elbow with theirs. "Later. For now, we find Grayson."

"Do you think he's with his mom?" Ace asked. "If he's not with his dad, he's got to be with his mom . . . and safe, right?"

No one needed to answer Ace's question. If it had been a good thing, Grayson would have said goodbye. There would have been some sign that he was okay.

"Is there any signal for him on that map?" Leo asked quietly.

Jayla was quiet for way too long. "There's a faint beacon that could be him. But it's far away. Really far."

"Let's go," Ace said, taking them even higher.

◻

Dr. Lance Bix knew all about Grayson trying to find his mom, Merrida. Every network search, every scan, every email. Only he hadn't actually been worried that his son would find her.

That would be impossible.

And yet, the boy had still disappeared right from between his fingers. No matter; he would find him. Cadets had already come forward with information following Emma's video, which he'd produced himself. They'd provided several leads. Not the least of which was the little rescue party that he'd let escape from the roof.

Dr. Bix lorded over his head office, using every secret security system to search for Grayson's whereabouts. Nothing so far. But even now he wasn't that worried.

Because Grayson had his aug now.

Coincidentally the best aug for tracking, VisionX.

It'd been a genius move to surround his son with the best and brightest, to encourage him to truly meet his potential and choose his aug. Even that favor he'd allowed concerning the Wells boy had worked out; Grayson had grown protective of the little pip. In Bix's experiments, he often built in controlling variables, and nothing left a person easier to control than caring for someone younger and weaker.

Dr. Bix squeezed his eyes tightly. It wasn't time for

another injection, but he was hurting for it. Tapping his tablet awake, he pulled up the holographic scan of Grayson taken when the boy was having his procedure. The scrolling text beside his son's image had all the details about Grayson's surgery and his file from his time at B.E.S.T., as well as other pertinent details about his life.

In the bottom left-hand corner, there was a small button that flashed slowly:

LIVE CAM

Even though it was for his own good, Grayson would never forgive him if he knew that Bix could see through his augmented eyes.

A knock on the door caused Bix to look up.

"Come in, Vaughn," he said. "News?"

"They took off in his hoverpod. They must know how to find him."

"That's good to hear."

Vaughn glanced at the tablet's holographic image and then away, quickly.

Bix closed the screen. "Problem, Vaughn?"

"Not at all."

The coach left, and Bix tried to relax, but he could only think about the ticking clock. The moment he'd get another injection of Bixonium and stave off his demise for a little longer. He opened the tablet again and pressed

Live Cam, and the tablet switched from showing Grayson's image to a blurry blue one.

"Come on, Grayson. Show me where you are . . ."

The image cleared, turning even bluer and endless.

Wherever Grayson Bix had been taken, he had the most beautiful view of the ocean.

PICK YOUR PERFECT AUG—BOD, BOOST, OR BRAIN

Aug Track: BOD

Where physical evolution is a *snap*

SuperSoar
Fly. Take off with style and glide on air currents for miles. Includes lighter bones and legit wings.

TurboLegs
Run as fast as the Hyperloop over great distances, no problem. Includes reinforced bones, joints, and ligaments.

VisionX
See colors you've never even heard of. Includes night vision and telescopic and microscopic zoom.

Hercules
Lift a hoverpod with one hand or do a thousand pull-ups without breaking a sweat. Includes reinforced bones, joints, and ligaments.

SonicBlast
Hear things no one else can or turn off annoying sounds—your choice. Includes new and improved echolocation.

HyperHops
Get the most powerful legs for jumping and swimming. Includes bonus joints and reinforced bones.

FelineFinesse
Never fall down again with a highly tuned sense of balance and increased spinal flexibility. Includes a tail, no joke.

Aug Track: BOOST

Where your natural strength gets *enhanced*

GillGraft

Breathe underwater for hours at a time. Includes new and improved internal decompression aid.

Scentrix

Super nose. Great taste. Increase your olfactory acuity. Includes new dampening mode to decrease sensitivity on demand.

UltraFlex

Be elastic, strong, and durable. Includes rubberized bones.

MegaMetabolism

Eat the whole cake or nothing at all. Survive in hazardous places with enhanced internal resilience. Includes an external gauge for switching between fasting and high-consumption modes.

SenseXL

Heighten all five senses at once. Become unstoppable. Includes new dampening mode to decrease sensitivity on demand.

DaVinci

Become your own muse with art as your first language. Includes superior dexterity and hand-eye coordination.

MetaMorph

Heal *fast*. Age slower and never get sick again. Includes improved cellular energy modifiers.

Aug Track: **BRAIN**
Where your mind becomes *unstoppable*

XConnect

Technology is your first language and fast friend. Includes an external interface for ease of transition and preliminary applications.

PassPort

Speak any language and master communication. Now includes several nonhuman languages such as dolphin, canine, and cricket.

NerveHack

Control your pain. Push your body to new levels without pesky nervous system restraints. Includes an external gauge for sensitivity transitions.

Mimic

Watch and learn; it's that easy. Includes increased mental storage to create your own database of abilities.

WeatherVein

Feel the tides, predict storms, and yes, catch lightning in a bottle. Includes rubberized bones for grounding during electrical atmospheric fluctuations.

Sherlock

Deduce, decode, and understand everything. Predict and detangle any mystery in a snap. Includes increased mental storage to create your own personalized database.

iNsight

Master the maze of human emotions. Achieve genius levels of emotional intelligence and empathetic influence. Now includes apathetic mode for on-demand sensitivity relief.

Acknowledgments

Special thanks to the great hearts and minds at HMH who invited me to an adventure on the coolest futuristic playground imaginable. In particular, thank you to my heroic boxmates: editor Chris Krones, agent Sarah Davies, spouse A. R. Capetta, and eternal inspiration Maverick.

TRAVEL TO ANOTHER WORLD WITH THESE MUST-READ

FANTASY BOOKS

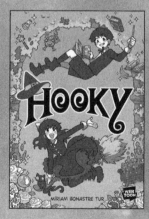

EXCITING
AND INSPIRING
STORIES

VERSIFY

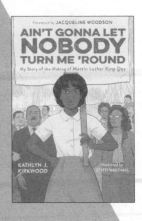

CHANGE THE WORLD, ONE WORD AT A TIME.